The Sustainers

By

Betty L. Alt

First published by Dog Ear Publishing
4011 Vincennes Rd
Indianapolis, IN 46268
www.dogearpublishing.net

ISBN: 978-1-4575-4519-1

This book is printed on acid-free paper.

This book is a work of fiction. Places, events, and situations in this book are purely fictional and any resemblance to actual persons, living or dead, is coincidental.

Printed in the United States of America

Prologue

"Food! Food! Food!" The cry echoed around the world in the twenty-first century as millions faced starvation. Changing weather patterns beginning in September and lasting until late March caused America's Great Lakes to almost completely freeze over; snowflakes fell briefly on southern Italy, inland Egypt, and parts of Brazil; ice appeared on the Thames River in England, and scientists predicted a worldwide 'mini ice age' would occur between 2030 and 2040. Around the globe during the brief summer, the scorching sun turned much originally fertile land into deserts in both the southern and northern hemispheres. Caught between the record-breaking cold and snow and worldwide drought, the growing season was cut each year to less than four months, and predictions were that the next world war would be fought over food.

For several years stockpiles of food in the industrial nations, particularly in the United States and Canada, helped to moderate the worsening food problem. Then in 2032, after the world's smallest harvest in over ten years, panic swept every nation, forcing governments to put aside political and military disagreements and concentrate on only one area – population survival. A Committee for Sustenance, composed of the sharpest agricultural and scientific minds in the world, was convened in Geneva and asked to study the looming crisis. After sixteen months — months filled with worldwide starvation and food riots — the committee's report was ready. Its predictions were catastrophic.

1. Unless food supplies could be increased astronomically, at least one third of the earth's total population would die of malnutrition or its effects within eight years.
2. The U.S., Canada, Australia, Argentina and other large cattle or grain-producing areas of the world could not continue to provide adequately for their own people let alone the population of other nations.
3. Immediate action was needed to reclaim and utilize for food production all land not needed for population housing.
4. To accomplish this, all populations should be moved, forcibly if necessary, into some form of immense high-rise cities. This would free for food production millions of suburban acreages presently utilized for such luxuries as single-family dwellings, lawns, swimming pools, patios, etc.

Acting on these dire recommendations, governments actively entered the field of agriculture and rigidly controlled all food supplies. The United States decided to concentrate its people into gigantic urban centers and to confiscate all other land for sustenance production. Private property ceased to exist.

The first tower — climbing toward the heavens instead of sprawling over land and with a population of nearly two million – was completed and occupied in February 2051, in what had been St. Louis. Chief architect for the project was the young, innovative George Stokes Benton who (with his wife Lucy Amos Benton and their young son, Amos) had personally surveyed the site as early as 2042. As the designer, Benton had the honor of naming the original tower. He suggested Babel-ON, a combination of the Biblical Tower of Babel and the hanging gardens of Babylon. His suggestion was accepted, and around the world towers were constructed – Eiffel-ON in Paris, Pisa-ON in Italy, the Tower of London (or the T of L as it was affectionately known).

In America, Benton had convinced the President, Congress, and many citizens that towers would "free up" needed space for food production. Cities as they had been known were razed; the work of survival began in earnest, and the entire population was relocated. Originally tower occupation had been through recruitment, and many had volunteered, mainly the young and venturesome who thrilled at being pioneers in a new concept of living and who willingly turned their suburban plots over to the government in exchange for a part of the future. (Among these were George and Lucy Benton who gave up their rural heritage and were among the first to enter Babel-ON.}

Included within each tower were schools, hospitals, shopping malls, theaters, recreational areas, living quarters – all of the necessities for life condensed into millions of fewer acres than the cities of old. A section devoted to industry and manufacturing was sealed off from other parts of the tower to avoid any chance of pollution or toxic gases reaching the otherwise ideal climatic conditions under which the population lived. Police and fire services were provided at intervals on various levels.

Intra-tower transportation in the form of elevators, escalators and moving sidewalks easily and quickly carried the workers or shoppers to their destinations. Air terminals were on the fringe of the tower for inter-tower or international transport. Highways and railroads connected towers to each other, and although at first some towerites had been permitted to take vacation tours to other towers on public transportation, this later was discouraged. Eventually all rails and roads were utilized solely for food transport. As a new generation grew up in the towers, fewer and fewer individuals ventured far from their birthplace. (It was estimated that by the year 2075, almost all populations in technologically developed areas would be born, would live, and would die without ever having left their towers.)

There were many in the American population, however, who balked at the idea of tower living. To counteract this, the government made it illegal to live outside a tower and forcibly moved those who tried to resist. Still, there were many problems and a period which came to be known as the "Cycle of Chaos" ensued. Suicide was high, especially among the elderly who felt they could not live "caged" up in a building. Black marketeering in food was rampant and took years to control; civil revolt developed in many areas with the government using the police, the National Guard, and military to quell the riots and enforce the laws. Thousands on both sides died during a period of nearly ten years – a time that became known as B.C. (Before Chaos) and A.C. (After Chaos). However, as food became scarcer and scarcer, people realized that survival meant tower living. By 2096, the U.S. tower system was functioning well, and people seemed to have adapted. As far as the government was concerned, no one could be living outside.

Chapter One

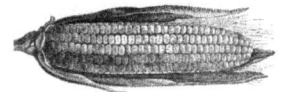

"A in't no animal done that, officer. When animals eat, there's always some leavin's. This was all done tidy." The woman stood with her hands on her hips, surveying the rows of corn which ran like green ribbons across the field and curled into the distance. "Went off toward the sump, they did," she continued as she pointed toward a mound of earth and limped forward, pushing the corn stalks away from her face.

Benton nodded to the man behind him, and they both began to follow her. Although it was early August, already the corn ears were full, and the stalks had the ragged look of harvest, their tassels frayed and drooping. Splotches of yellow and brown dulled the brittle green leaves.

The woman moved swiftly despite the limp, her worn oxfords raising dust as she dragged one shoe to favor her right leg. She was old but just how old was hard to tell. *Probably in her late sixties* Benton thought. That would make her, like him, part of the pre-tower population. However, she would have lived more than half of her life before Babel-ON existed, while he had been eleven years old when his family had left the outside. He would have liked to question her about the earlier years, but his partner, Shaner, might misunderstand, might even feel it was something to be reported. He and Bill Shaner had worked closely together for seventeen months and had become good friends, sharing a mutual respect for each other's ability and dedication to the job; yet, somehow Benton knew that Shaner's loyalty to Babel-ON and the new social order was much stronger than his own. Shaner might wonder at Benton's interest in earlier times. Besides, the old woman would be perfectly justified in taking offense if he asked questions, and she, too, might report him.

Still he noted the split heels on the oxfords and the faded stockings that stretched tightly over swollen ankles. Benton wondered if her limp was the result of the enlarged right leg or whether it might be due to some old injury. She wore the shapeless green and white coveralls of most of the agricultural population but with the pant legs rolled almost to her knees. Benton did not see many old people any more as a substantial number had died during "Chaos." Babel-ON and the other towers were chiefly populated by the youth of the country. *She is one of the more fortunate ones* he mused. *She is still with us because she is a sustainer.*

"Ate their supper up there, officer." The old woman turned and pointed to the bank. "You gimme a hand and we'll look it over." Benton extended his hand and began to pull her up the sloping ground. Her skin was hot and rough to the touch, he noted, and the grasp was firm. Shaner scrambled up the bank first and gave a shout of surprise. "Hey! There's a lake."

"Ain't a lake, officer. Just a watering pond from when we used to have livestock here. But it is pretty fair size. Catches the run-off, and there may be a spring at the far end. My daddy used to know, but I forget what he told me." She was panting a little, and a drop of perspiration oozed out of the gray hair and moved slowly down her cheek. "Been a long, long time . . ."

Stopping abruptly, the woman bent over and picked up a corn cob, handing it to Shaner as she kicked at some withered pieces of husk. "Shucked it cleaner 'n a whistle. Ain't no animal done that. Had to be human." She turned and faced Benton squarely, her arm raised to cut the glare of the sun from her eyes. "What human in his right mind would dare steal corn these days, officer? And, who could possibly be living outside?"

"First of all, Mrs. Yates, we're not officers — not police officers, if that's what you mean." It had been years since Benton had heard the term "officer." There were no policemen now as there had been in the old days; now they were called "guides." It was their duty to guide any deviants back into the accepted ways of the society. Of course, if the offender refused or if it were a major offense, the guide could use force for the good of the population. It was rumored that this force could be extremely brutal, and there were whispers about secret penal institutions, but as far as Benton knew, they were just that — whispers and rumors.

"Mr. Shaner and I are with the Bureau of Sustenance . . . sort of like the old . . . county agricultural agents . . ." Benton groped for words to make her understand. "We are sent out from Babel-ON to educate sustainers to better farm methods or to investigate any irregularities in the food production of an area. Therefore when you called about a raid on this corn field . . ."

3

"Raids," she interrupted. "I called now for three, maybe four years. Get a few raids right around this time for the last four years. Didn't bother me much the first time or two as I figured it was some animal, but now there's more and more corn gone with each raid. How'm I gonna explain the loss to the Bureau? They expect that those of us working these acres will supply a certain amount of product, and I'm the one always making the repots." She stopped and shook her head. "The Bureau don't seem to understand much about us sustainers. I don't want no trouble."

"Yes, we're aware that you reported various incidents previously, Mrs. Yates." Benton found it difficult not to smile at the implied criticism of the Bureau. She was a plain-speaking old woman, something rare these days. "The Bureau will have made a notation to expect some shortages in production from this acreage until we solve the puzzle."

"Well, I should hope so," she snorted as she began to descend toward the rows of corn. "Look around all you want. I'm going to be over near the far fence where my home used to be. Still have a shell of a house over there. Keeps you dry when there's a hard rain. I'll fix you fellows some fresh corn for lunch. The Bureau can add it to my other losses."

Benton nodded to Shaner to go with her. "See if you can help her out, Bill. She doesn't walk too steadily, and she might remember something else that could help us. Also you might keep your eyes open as you head toward that end of the field. I'll circle the sump and see if there's any indication of what's causing all of this."

Shaner grinned and set off after Mrs. Yates, who was already out of sight, only a rustling sound and slight movement in the tall corn to indicate her progress. After Shaner left, Amos

Benton walked slowly to a grove of trees at the pond's far end. There he found a number of corn cobs and husks and some drying pea pods. He wondered if Mrs. Yates had a small garden near her old house. It was legal if she did; many of the older sustainers, whose families at one time had owned their land, were permitted to do so as long as they were actively in the fields working for the Bureau. He would bet the pea vines had also been stripped by her "visitors."

Obviously, they, whoever they were, had stopped in the shelter of the trees to eat, apparently hungry enough to risk possibly being seen or captured. Even if the theft had occurred at night, they might still be in some danger of being seen by someone in a food transport on its way to Babel-ON. Benton agreed with the old woman. Whoever had taken the food was human. But who? And from where? Someone living outside of the towers in these days! That was impossible with the screening process which has been used by the government. Where did they hide . . . where could they hide?

As he looked out in the distance, Benton was met by the sight of endless rows of corn. A quarter of a mile away he thought he could make out a fence and more corn fields stretching to the horizon. "Wonder if the next field was raided?" he said aloud and decided that it should be checked out before a final report was handed in to the Bureau.

It was pleasant among the trees. A slight breeze ruffled his dark hair which was beginning to show a touch of gray at the temples. Leaning against a trunk, he looked across the water, watching the sun shimmering like glass on the smooth surface. He could hear sounds of insects and noted a hawk in the distance, lazily floating in the cloudless sky. The heat of the August sun was somewhat dissipated by the breeze, and the nearby foliage was mirrored in the glare of the water. Close to the water's edge was a large clump of day lilies, their orange blossoms delicately balanced atop thin stems and entwined with coiling leaves. A dragon fly briefly glided close to the water's surface and then flitted away. The whole scene reminded Benton of an oriental painting he had seen once on a visit to Babel-ON's art museum, a visit he had made to fulfill a block on his cultural learning chart.

Amos Benton sighed, for what reason he didn't fully know. Perhaps it was for the beauty of the day or for the nearly forgotten memory of some earlier day of beauty. This was the major reward of his job, that he could get out of Babel-ON and see again the wonder of nature – something his ancestors had taken for granted – the ability to travel freely around the countryside; to move at least for a few hours back to their rural roots; to see a tree; to lie for a day in the sun; to dig in the earth.

"Ohhh, dangerous thoughts, Benton," he said, as he edged back around the pond. How good everything smelled; how alive and well he felt. It was difficult to realize on this warm August afternoon that by the second week in September snow would begin to fall and put an end to the growing season. Sustainers everywhere were racing against time to try and avert the catastrophe of earlier years when food had been in short supply.

He thought of old Mrs. Yates and envied her this place, even though it was no longer hers. How he wished, for an instance, that he were a sustainer like her rather than just an employee in the area of sustenance. However, he knew this was impossible. Only the children or relatives of sustainers were now permitted to work the land. In fact, they were required to do so rather than move into other areas of employment. He smiled. Probably somewhere there was a sustainer who would have given anything to change places with him – a sustainer who wanted desperately to live in Babel-On and be a member of the Bureau. He laughed aloud, the sound startling a covey of quail. Watching their flight until they resettled, he shrugged and moved from the sump down into the cornfield.

Suddenly, he felt something was watching him. Slowing his stride, he casually stooped and brushed some dust from his trouser leg. As he straightened up, he turned slightly and surveyed the rows of corn behind him. Nothing! He shrugged. A faint rustling sound could be, probably was, only a small animal or the corn stalks nodding against each other in the slight breeze. Benton moved closer to a row and peered among the leaves, his pale blue eyes searching for the source of the sound. Nothing! Again he shrugged and moved on. *You're as edgy as the old woman* he thought, but the uneasy feeling would not leave him. As he made his way through the corn rows, he glanced several times back over his shoulder only to see – nothing.

As he entered her house, Benton saw that Mrs. Yates had a big kettle set on an old wood stove in the corner of the kitchen. When she saw him, she popped several ears of corn into the boiling water. "Didn't want to start 'em 'til you came. Corn's no good if it cooks over long."

He noticed that she had set three pale blue plates, all of them chipped, on a rickety table. Shaner came in carrying two pails of water from the well, a sheepish grin on his face as he set the pails down and brushed a lock of auburn hair from his forehead. "She'll make a sustainer out of you yet, Bill," Benton joked, clearing a spot for the containers.

"Not me," Shaner protested. "Wide open space gives me the creeps. No offense, ma'am," he added as he saw Mrs. Yates turn and stare at him.

"None taken," the old woman replied, "only I get a creepy feeling in my sub-tower, and it ain't near big as Babel-On or some o' those others. Ain't natural, people being cooped up inside all their born days, everybody living atop everybody else. Whole world's gone crazy . . ."

"It's necessary, ma'am," Shaner interrupted. "People have to have sustenance. Land must be maintained first and foremost for food production. Everything else is secondary." His voice rose, Benton noticed, as he warmed to his subject matter. "The Bureau of Sustenance has made exhaustive studies and has found it absolutely necessary to utilize the towers for overall better living conditions and the overall well-being . . ."

"Well, what's necessary is necessary, I guess." The old woman interrupted as she turned back to the boiling corn, "But it ain't my idea of living nor well-being."

Shaner glanced at Benton, a puzzled look on his face. Mrs. Yates was making statements that could cause her a great deal of trouble, could cause her to be removed as a sustainer, if the Bureau thought her enough of a troublemaker. Benton smiled at Shaner and winked, indicating for him to drop the subject.

"Ain't got no butter; ain't had none for over four years. This salt may help a little." She handed an old metal salt shaker to Benton and began fishing the steaming ears of corn from the pot. "Still, what's corn without a big pat of butter?"

It had been over twenty years since Benton had eaten corn on the cob, and Shaner never had done so. Food in

Babel-On and the other towers was nutritious and appetizing, but it came processed into wafers which expanded with cooking. A good cook could, with a little imagination, turn out tempting dishes from the wafers. However, the food never took on the appearance of its original form nor the mouth-watering aroma from this food which was bringing back to Benton long-dead memories that made him uncomfortable.

Benton salted the corn and bit into the succulent kernels, showing Shaner how to hold the steaming cob. After the first mouthful Shaner had a surprised look on his face and then smiled appreciatively at Mrs. Yates. They ate in silence for a few minutes, savoring the freshness of the food and rarity of the opportunity. Benton had not realized that he was hungry, but he ate without stopping until the fourth ear of corn disappeared. He wiped his mouth with the back of his hand, brushing salt onto his uniform. "I can see why they steal your corn, Mrs. Yates. I almost envy them."

Shaner stopped eating and looked from Benton to the old woman, his dark eyes questioning. *He doesn't know what to think* Benton mused. *He can't be certain if what we are doing or saying isn't illegal. If we are illegal, then so is he.* Benton laughed to reassure Shaner that he had been joking and settled back to wait while the other two finished eating.

They stayed only a little longer — long enough to help the old woman extinguish the fire in the stove and to check the other rooms for any evidence of illegal habitation. The house had been large but unpretentious and was badly in need of repair as the ceilings were sagging and the floors wobbly. Other than the kitchen, there was a dining room ("Something almost obsolete these days," Benton noted to Shaner), a living room with a small fireplace, a tiny room that might have served as a bedroom, and a bathroom.

"Toilet would still work if I could get electricity to turn the pump on," Mrs. Yates explained. "Has a septic tank and leeching field. Every now and then I long to take a real bath again, in a real bathtub like this one, not one of those things we have to use in the tower."

The house contained little furniture with the exception of that in the kitchen and a cot in the dining room, its iron frame showing spots of rust through chipped brown paint. In the bedroom was a small vanity, ornately carved, but with a brick helping to prop up one side where a leg was missing. One of its folding three-way mirrors had a broken section, but the glass was surprisingly clean. A box of powder sat on one corner near a bottle of amber liquid and a faded picture of a young man. The vanity stool was a wooden box placed squarely in front of the largest mirror. Benton wondered if the old woman regularly sat there and what she thought about as she stared at her reflection.

A large screened porch, badly in need of repair, surrounded two sides of the house, its once dark brown boards and white trim faded and peeling. From the porch a broken cement walk curved among knee-high weeds toward a dilapidated privy and an open gate which dangled by one hinge. Benton could hear the faint clatter of branches on the porch roof from an immense tree that stood nearby.

I stay here some nights," Mrs. Yates explained. "No one seems to give me trouble about that although I know I'm supposed to stay in the sustainer quarters. But they're so confining, and then I'm so much older than most of the others . . ." Her words trailed off.

Benton and Shaner had seen the sustainer sub towers earlier as they drove between the fields. Squat, painted green, they were universally constructed of a plastic material impervious to the heat of summer and to the below zero temperatures which gripped the land for eight months of each year. Sustainers lived in the quarters only during the growing season, returning to larger sustainer towers which were similar to but much smaller than those like Babel-ON. Benton could easily understand why Mrs. Yates preferred her old house, even though the floors sagged badly and the sky could be seen through some rather large places in the roof.

"Evening breeze is getting stronger," he murmured. "We'd better be heading back to Babel-ON, Bill, although I did want to check out the fields down the road."

Both men thanked the old woman for her hospitality and moved out into the yard. Benton gazed off toward the sump. "We may be back out in a few days, Mrs. Yates, to see if anything new has developed and to look around the neighboring land." The three of them stopped at the edge of the corn field.

"I'll see if I can round up some more corn," she laughed, looking at Shaner. "I'll make you wish you were a sustainer yet."

Benton waved and followed Shaner into the rows of corn, back toward where their vehicle was parked. Again he had the eerie feeling of being watched but noticed that Shaner was apparently unaware of anything out of the ordinary. Benton started to say something and then decided not to. His imagination must be playing tricks on him.

It took nearly five minutes to reach the Bureau truck which was parked on one of the main farm arteries that transported sustenance from agricultural areas to the towers. There was no traffic in sight, but they didn't expect any. Arteries were maintained in excellent condition solely for food transport and other occasionally necessary travel. Personal vehicles had been banned for decades. Very limited mass transportation was available; however, fewer and fewer people traveled beyond their own tower, most reaching maturity without ever having been outside the tower in which they were born.

"She sure said a lot of funny things," Shaner began as he settled his wiry frame back in the truck's seat and lowered the window to get rid of the stale air. Lots of people in the Bureau would be upset if they had heard her."

Benton waited until the vehicle had picked up speed before he replied. He didn't want to appear too anxious to defend Mrs. Yates. He especially didn't want Shaner suspicious of both him and the old woman. "Well, Bill, you've got to realize that she's old, maybe getting a little senile."

Shaner nodded in agreement. "Yeah, I think I heard something about that happening to old people. I've never seen many old people close up, but I remember one of my teachers told us something about that when we were in school."

"Then, too," Benton continued, "she probably lived a long time outside when things were quite different . . . not better, of course," Benton was quick to add, "but she had a lot of adjustment to make. Take us for instance. I came to Babel-ON as a young boy, and you were born there. You don't know anything different, and I can't remember much about former times."

That wasn't true, Benton knew, but it sounded good. Actually he wished he could forget his pre-tower days, but as he grew older, he seemed to recall more of the events of his first years than he could of his immediate past. What was worse, he liked what he could recall and was saddened that his life would never be that way again. He had enjoyed this day and would push to be able to go back out again.

"I'm sure there are a few other sustainers who are old and live in ramshackle places outside a sustainer tower part of the year, and the Bureau doesn't seem to care," he continued. "You must admit that Mrs. Yates was interesting," Benton looked over at Shaner, "and I'm sure she's harmless."

"Yeah, what's one old lady anyway," Shaner concluded, "but it could do a lot of damage if everyone thought like she does."

They drove on in companionable silence, the fields of sustenance stretching out for miles on either side. At dusk they neared the Mississippi. Already they could see the lights of Babel-ON miles away on the horizon. It wasn't a homecoming for Benton, but he knew he had to keep his thoughts to himself.

Chapter Two

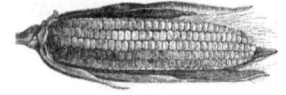

*T*he boy raced through the corn rows. *Wait till I tell Margot* he thought. He had watched the men all afternoon, staying with the one at the pond and then waiting patiently while both were in the house with the old woman. He had even followed them to the artery and watched until their dark green vehicle had disappeared from sight, its stalks of ripe grain clutched in grasping hands emblazoned on each door. He knew he should not have gone that far. Margot would be very angry with him as he had been warned repeatedly never to go far from the haven. He had meant only to go a short way into the fields, hoping to find some wild berries or wild asparagus, even though it would be old and tough at this time of year. Finding a few berries, he had eaten them immediately, not saving any for the others. With feelings of guilt, he had searched farther and farther until he had heard the three people moving through the corn.

Once he thought he had been discovered, but he had lain completely still, holding his breath. One of the men had sensed something but after peering into the corn rows had moved on. Outside the house the boy had waited for what seemed like hours, hidden in some thick currant bushes. Several ants had bitten him and, as the evening breeze became stronger, his thin shirt did little to protect him from the evening chill. He was cold. He was hungry and his stomach ached. But the currants were not fully ripe yet, and he knew not to eat them. The memory of other days when the mothers had prepared hot soup came to his mind and caused him to salivate. However, that was before the accident, before his life had changed to this time of always being hungry. He longed for something warm in his stomach and hoped that Margot might feel it safe to have a fire. Even a cup of hot water would make him feel good.

Now as he neared the haven, he became even more excited. "Wait 'til I tell Margot," he panted aloud. "She'll see I can help out. I'm not a kid any more. I can help take care of the others. I'm big enough now to be counted in talk times."

The boy knew there were many problems, but Margot and Michael always put on a calm face around him and the other younger ones. Of course, some things Margot talked about he didn't understand fully, but as he grew older and watched more carefully, his understanding grew. He knew Robin was going to have a baby for everyone was concerned that she have an extra ration of food. He wasn't too sure about babies, and whenever he questioned Margot or Michael about the subject, they always turned his attention to other things. He had also heard Margot mention to Michael that they needed more men – for Lauren and Noreen. He hadn't liked that. Margot and Michael always thought of him as their little brother, but he was a man. He and Michael were all the men that were needed. They could take care of the others; they didn't need more men.

"Wait 'til I tell Margot," he said aloud again. "I'll bet this is something she doesn't know for once." Momentarily he slowed his running as the path was uneven, and he didn't want to trip and fall. *Surely Margot wouldn't know about the two men* he reasoned, *although she seems to have some uncanny sense of awareness about anything that might affect our group.* Once, Robin had told him that the elves whispered secrets to Margot at night, but he didn't believe that any more. Still, how she knew so much that the others didn't baffled him. However, this time he would surprise her. He began to speed up his pace. Just a few more minutes and he would be able to spot the entrance to the haven.

"Two men in uniforms again. Are you sure they wore uniforms?"

"Margot, I told you – two men – I saw them; I followed them." The boy tugged at her arm in agitation.

"Calm down, Jamie. Sit here." She pulled him into a faded orange plastic chair, its back propped against the concrete wall. "Tell me again, right from the start. What did they do? Could you hear what they said?"

The boy recounted the afternoon's events, ending lamely. "I couldn't hear much 'cause I couldn't get close enough." He didn't want Margot angry because he had risked being caught. "They didn't seem very upset – just poked around in the corn and by the pond. They did find the corn cobs. You know, Margot, we shouldn't leave those around."

Margot looked across at a young man who had been listening intently to the conversation. As their eyes met, he raised one eyebrow but said nothing when she agreed. "You're right,

Jamie. We'll try not to be so careless again." Actually she and Michael had made certain the corn cobs would be left in obvious places.

"I brought back some good news, didn't I? You didn't know those men were here looking around, did you?"

"No, Jamie. You did well. It was lucky you were there so we could be alerted, but you need to be more careful." She put her hand on his shoulder and squeezed gently. He was their younger brother. "Michael and I are quite pleased with you."

For the first time, the man spoke, echoing the woman's words. "I'm sure Margot will ask for your help again, Jamie, and I want you to know that I'm proud of my little brother. Now, call the others as we will be eating soon, and, oh, yes, don't mention this to the others. Not yet. Later we can tell them what you found out."

Jamie looked from Michael to Margot, his blue eyes questioning. He had so wanted to let the others know that he had acted correctly, that he was an important part of the group. "Okay, if you say so, I guess." He shuffled his feet, shifting his gaze to the floor.

"We have to keep secrets sometimes, for the ease of the others," Margot began. "We don't want everyone worried or frantic, do we? You're thirteen now and can take on more responsibility." Soon, she knew, she would have to tell him and the others of the critical situation they were all facing.

"Is it a hot dinner, Margot?"

"No, Jamie. I was afraid to have a fire with the sustainers in the field. Still, since the men from the tower probably have gone by now, and the sustainers soon will be going to their huts for the night, we'll risk enough fire for some hot tea. Now do as Michael said and get the others."

As the boy left the room, she glanced at Michael. "I think maybe our plan finally is going to work. I'm sure the Bureau will send those two men back to make a more thorough investigation of the disappearance of the corn, and we've got to be ready if they do."

Michael began moving chairs over to a large table. "Does it matter if it isn't the same two men?"

"Not at all. Any men will do nicely."

Chapter Three

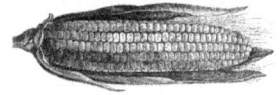

“ *H* e's waiting for you two," the secretary smiled as she nodded toward a door lettered in green: MANAGER, P. P. D.

Benton knew he would be waiting. The Bureau of Sustenance was operated on a twenty-four-hour basis, holidays and Sundays no exception. The production of food was a twenty-four-hour necessity if the massive world population was to be kept from further malnutrition and starvation, not to mention the most dreaded possibilities of all – revolt and war. Even those with positions of rank such as Managers and Directors usually could be found putting in extra hours, hoping that their presence would alleviate or at least aid in solving any problems that might arise. Solomon John, Manager of Benton and Shaner's section of Production, Processing and Distribution (PPD), had the reputation for always having his finger on the controls.

The manager, a tall, thin, black haired man with nervous hands and an officious manner, rose to meet the two men as they entered his office. "You were gone longer that I anticipated." He motioned them to chairs in front of his desk and then sat down. "Have some unforeseen problems?"

Benton took his time getting settled, waiting to see if Shaner would respond. "I thought it took an awfully long time myself," Shaner began with a quick laugh. "Those cornfields don't exactly offer one companionship." He smiled at Solomon John who did not return the smile.

Totally humorless Benton thought. *They should have named him Solemn John.*

"What do you have to report?" John switched his gaze to Benton and began straightening papers on his desk, its mahogany top polished to a high gloss.

"Not much," Benton replied. "Walked all over that farm. Pretty fair size. Found where they had stopped to eat the corn, but no sign of anything moving out there 'cept a few birds."

"Did you see anything?" John pinpointed Shaner.

"No! Course I went back with the old woman to her home . . ."

"Her home?" The manager raised his eyebrows so that they stood out blackly above his dark-rimmed glasses. He had never approved of sustainers being permitted to be outside of sustainer huts during the growing season. "A **tower** is her home!"

"What used to be her home, I guess," Shaner corrected uneasily. "It's an old rundown place where she has a little garden and where she goes to rest from the sun. She can't work as long as some other sustainers. She's an old lady, you know."

"No, I didn't know!" Solomon John emphasized the words. The Bureau just has her recent letter and notations on several calls she made over the past few years. I haven't bothered to check her records. What did you do at the house?"

"Only checked it out for her to make sure no one was hiding around it," Shaner answered. "Also, she has a sore foot and couldn't walk very well, so I went along to make sure she got there while Benton checked out the lake."

"Sump," Benton corrected. "They left from the sump, maybe going to another field. That's only my guess, of course." He noted that Shaner had neglected to mention the fresh corn the old woman had cooked for them. "Either that or they wanted a picturesque view with their dinner."

Again Solomon John did not smile. "They? Do you infer 'they' to be human?"

"I'm afraid so . . ." Benton began.

"Impossible!" John broke in. "Impossible! Where could they go? Where could they hide? Who could they be? We certainly have accounted for all of the human population in the United States."

"I'm hoping you're right, sir." Benton slipped in the term of respect, knowing it would please his supervisor. "However, the Bureau didn't oversee the population survey ourselves. The demography section did that. I'm not throwing any stones mind you, but I'm not sure they are as thorough as we are since they don't have to bother about actually feeding the population. That burden falls on us. We have that responsibility, and it's a responsibility that seems to be getting bigger and bigger what with a good portion of the rest of the world not able to produce much food yet." He stopped, shifted his position. "If they are out there . . ." He let the implication hang.

"Yes, if they are, we may have trouble. We haven't had any sightings for several years now, and we haven't had a sighting at all of this bunch, if it is a bunch." Solomon John paused, wrinkling his nose in apparent distaste at the words "trouble" and "bunch." He gazed into space for a few minutes, as if to try and come to grips with what he had been saying, and then swung his eyes back to Benton. "But we can't go on **ifs**, Benton."

Benton nearly sighed with relief. John had paved the way for his next comment. "True, you can't go upstairs with that – to the Director." He waited a minute before adding in a subdued, somewhat offhand manner. "Possibly we could come up with something more concrete for you."

Again Benton waited. To suggest that he and Shaner return to the fields was out of the question. Solomon John did not take kindly to any suggestions – particularly from those who worked for him. He was the type of man who had all of the answers, who considered himself above his fellow workers in reasoning ability. His manner and his tone of voice always held a hint of condescension. John continued to shuffle papers on his desk, his long, thin fingers darting over the pages. "You two may have to go back out there again, look further, bring me some proof. Then I'll go to the Director. But it's got to be proof – no suppositions – you hear?"

Benton nodded. "You must mean us to stay out more than a day then. Can't fly or drive out there, see anything and get back to Babel-ON by dark. Fact is, we'd probably see more at night, if there's anything to see. That's when the foraging seems to happen. Don't know where we'd stay though, since the closest sub-tower's several miles away. Weather could be a major factor also as winter's approaching. Guess we could stay in a sustainer hut along with the others working where the old woman is, but they might begin to wonder why we were there. I don't imagine you want a great deal of speculation over what's happening."

"Definitely not," John responded. "Keep all of this quiet, you hear?"

Both Benton and Shaner nodded that they understood and waited for John to continue. "Why not stay in the house – the old lady's house? You'd have a bit of shelter and yet know of anything or anyone rummaging in the fields." John nodded to himself in satisfaction now that the lodging arrangements were finalized. He knew that shelter of some kind could be vitally important in case of sudden drops in temperature which were now common in large portions of the northern hemisphere. As sustainer sub-towers were widely scattered, to get marooned from mid-September to late May any distance from a tower meant almost certain death if an individual was not fully prepared and trained for the emergency. "Don't scrimp on supplies and be sure you're thorough with this investigation."

Benton was so elated he thought he was going to laugh aloud. He had hoped to return, to get out of Babel-ON once again, to see the sump and the fields, to go back in time at least for a few more hours. As calmly as possible he said, "Good idea. That okay with you, Shaner?"

Shaner shrugged indifferently. "Back to the cornfields, I guess."

Benton studied his partner's face but couldn't tell what Shaner was thinking. Coming in from the trip he had complained about the "creepy fields" and mumbled about how impossible it must be to try and exist without a guaranteed food supply and the comfort and security of a tower. Now he seemed unusually low key. Did he want to go back outside again, or was he just afraid to voice any objections to Solomon John? *Maybe he wants some more corn on the cob* Benton thought but knew that was too simple an answer.

"Very well. I'll clear it with the Director's office for you to be gone at least a week. Weather should not be a problem for a week, but not longer than that," Solomon John stated. "Probably better plan on day after tomorrow at the earliest." Before he dismissed them, he added, "Let your families know," and then remembered, too late, that Benton's wife had suffered some severe emotional problems nearly six years earlier and had been in the tower's Custodial Care facility ever since. Shaner looked a little uneasy, but Benton gave no sign that he had heard the remark. "Well, at any rate," Solomon John said as he concluded the meeting, "better draw adequate rations or you won't have anything at all to eat out there."

Benton met Shaner's eyes, and they became partners in their silence.

Chapter Four

𝒯he two sustainers left the Bureau office and made their way toward their respective living quarters. Main business sections on the lower floors were sparsely populated at the late hour, but Benton and Shaner knew that several levels above the evening recreational activities would be drawing huge crowds. Although the tower designers, including Benton's father, had attempted to create an atmosphere of freedom and space, the living quarters of the average family were minuscule compared to those of United States suburbanites in the latter half of the twentieth century and the first four decades of the twenty-first. Therefore, family energies which formerly had been channeled into long distance errands, yard maintenance, housekeeping, etc., found little release in tower living.

Even television could not fill the excess leisure time, and Benton remembered statistics from the first few years of tower life which showed great increases in marital discord, juvenile delinquency, violent crime, emotional illness and suicide as people attempted to adjust to the more confined lifestyle. Government programs, on a voluntary basis, had been started in all areas of sports, entertainment and education, and the population had been encouraged to participate after the normal working hours. When these voluntary programs were met with apathy by many people, they ceased being voluntary. Each citizen was required to participate in a minimum of three leisure activities weekly, which had somewhat alleviated the problem of too much idle time. As generations were born and grew to adulthood within the tower system, socialized to the closeness and enforced rigidity of tower living and never having known the freedom of living outside, most of the earlier social problems tended to decline. Out of necessity, tower living had become the only acceptable way of life.

Benton and Shaner had both selected a physical fitness program, first because it was required and secondly because being physically fit helped them if, like today, they had to tramp about the countryside inspecting or estimating the anticipated food supply. Since Solomon John's division in the Bureau was a large one, inspection trips were rotated among the many personnel. Benton had not been outside Babel-ON for nearly a year, and Shaner had been outside only once before during his training period.

Now, as the elevator stopped at the thirty-ninth floor, they got off and moved through the foot traffic to an escalator which lifted them four additional floors to a large swimming pool and gym facility. It was just one of several hundred pools in the tower and for some reason usually was less congested than those much higher up in the complex.

"I'm not going to the concert tonight," Benton told Shaner, "as I need to see Martha and then do some thinking on this new assignment we have. Need to make up a list of supplies to tide us over."

Shaner's eyes met his but, like Solomon John, he did not comment on nor ask about Martha Benton. "How long we gonna be out there?"

Benton couldn't read the expression on Shaner's face. Was it anxiety? Was it merely questioning? Was it a little too intense? "Three, maybe four days probably." He paused and stared hard at his partner. Perhaps the emptiness of the fields really had frightened him. After all, unlike Benton, Shaner only knew tower life. "Could be longer, though. Would you rather not go? I could get John to assign someone else, or I could go alone."

"No! No, I'm as anxious as you to see what's out there eating the old woman's corn. Besides, it will be sort of like one of those adventure films we always see. Come on. Let's get into the pool while it's still relatively empty."

They had enjoyed the swim, and later Shaner had joined some friends to go on to the concert. Benton made his way up three additional floors to one of the tower's green areas – a small section extending out into space from the basic wall structure, with fountains and plastic benches tucked among the foliage. Selecting a seat away from the few discreetly placed lights and out of the general traffic pattern, Benton sniffed the air. Only the odor of a well-tended greenhouse was noticeable. He remembered the smell of the sun on the corn and wished he could recall from earlier times the odors of nightfall as the evening sun set and the summer earth cooled. "Enough of that daydreaming, Benton," he chided himself aloud. "Get busy on the list of supplies."

Sleeping gear, field equipment for meals, at least a week's ration of food, first aid kit, heavy clothing in case the night dropped to freezing, flashlights (heavy duty ones), pistols and rifles. He stared at the last words on the list. Was he expecting danger? Would he actually use the weapons, even if there were non-sustainers? He could not recall when he had last heard of anyone being shot – seven years, no, closer to twelve. Finally, he added a large amount of butter substitute to his list, just in case the old woman fixed corn again.

An approaching couple caught his eye. "Evening," Benton nodded, noting that both were graying and estimating their ages at around sixty. He thought of the bit of gray in his own hair, and he was only forty-nine.

"Nice night," the man responded, and the woman smiled timidly as they moved along the simulated flagstone path to nearby seats. They didn't talk, Benton noticed, only sat quietly, and once the woman reached out and touched a bush, as if making certain it was not synthetic. She drew her hand back quickly and laughed as the man clucked to her, "Now, now. Shouldn't touch. We have plants at home."

Benton reflected on the man's words about it being a nice night. It was true. It was a nice night. It was **always** a nice night in the tower, although one only knew it was night by the tower clocks and the dimming of the "second sun," that light from the sun which was diffused throughout the tower by the reflection from strategically placed huge mirrors. The temperature remained constant; the humidity was always at the right level; the wind never shuffled dead leaves along the corridors of Babel-ON. It was always a nice night; it was always a nice day. A restless feeling descended on Benton, a feeling of disquiet – a feeling he couldn't quite define. Remembering Solomon John's remark about letting their families know about their proposed sojourn outside, Benton knew he would have to visit his wife, although the visit would bring no pleasure to either of them. Her deep depression required that she be kept in psychiatric care.

"Thought an old man like you would have been in bed an hour ago." Shaner suddenly appeared on the path, clutching the hand of a dark-haired girl, her face attractively framed with soft curls.

"Not so old I can't take you on any day," Benton countered with the expected banter as he stood up. "How was the concert, Lana?" He smiled, gazing into the girl's hazel eyes.

"Very good, actually, Mr. Benton," Lana Howard replied as she returned the smile. "But I guess you're going to leave me without an escort for a while from what Bill tells me."

"I'll bring him back to you in about a week unless he decides to become a sustainer."

"Not a chance. I'm glad my dad came inside as one of the earlier ones," Shaner laughed, and the couple bid Benton goodnight.

Benton watched the two walk away, arm in arm, laughing together. He sighed. Once Martha and he had been like that, in love, the sexual attraction strong and vital. Somehow he couldn't remember anything specific about their love or marriage. It was as though it hadn't existed. For an instant he was wildly envious of Shaner, envious of the feeling of anticipation at seeing, being with a loved one. He wondered if his wife occasionally felt as he did, was even able to feel as he did. Well, he would briefly visit her, see if there were any improvement. Nearly an hour later, as he rode up to the Custodial Care Center on the eighty-sixth floor, Benton felt a sudden sense of elation. He could deal with his personal problems later. Day after tomorrow he would get to go outside again.

Chapter Five

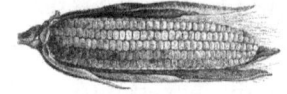

*W*alking through the halls of the C. C. C., Benton thought it odd that with all of the scientific and medical progress being made in the latter days of the 21ˢᵗ century, mental illness still existed. He could feel the sense of hopelessness in spite of the Custodial Care Center's decorating efforts to project a feeling of brightness and comfort. Pastel yellow walls were dotted with baskets of artificial flowers or hung with artistic works. Comfortable furniture was strategically placed, and each cubicle was designed to give some little privacy. Scurrying to and fro were a number of doctors and an abundance of attendants, unlike the twentieth century when care for those with emotional illness tended to be haphazard and inadequate. Of course, as Benton knew, during the Time of Chaos those who became emotionally unstable or suffered suicidal tendencies were pretty much ignored as the resources of the government had to be directed to regaining stability in life for those able to cope with a rapidly changing world. Martha Benton was at least fortunate that her illness had not become acute earlier.

"Severe depression," the psychiatrist had originally told Benton.

"What does that mean exactly?" Benton had questioned. "In terms of treatment, I mean, or in terms of time?"

"Depends. She could be like this for years, or she could snap out of it overnight. To be honest, it doesn't look like she'll snap out of it soon. I've been working with her now for nearly a year, and I can't seem to reach her, don't seem to be making much progress with her treatment. As you know I've called in Dr Williams as a consultant, but he doesn't report any change either."

"The child . . . ," Benton began.

"Could be, but I doubt it. Apparently she went through a normal mourning period and then moved on with her life. You two never had another child though, did you?"

"Uh, no," Benton met the doctor's gaze. "Not that we didn't want one . . ." He let the words die away. *Actually that wasn't true he thought. He hadn't wanted another child, hadn't wanted to create a new little towerite. If there hadn't been such a huge world population in the latter part of the last century, the world would not literally still be starving to death. He could recall the television programs showing thousands in Africa, the children with skeletal limbs and huge distended bellies, lying in makeshift hospital tents. Nearby an emaciated female would be giving birth – giving birth to a son or daughter that only faced a future of starvation. Had Martha known that he felt this way? He had never talked about these feelings with her. Had she somehow known anyway? Was this what had caused her to withdraw into herself? No! He refused to accept the implied guilt.*

"We tried to be happy," Benton continued defensively. "Just the two of us, but gradually she became disinterested in life – detached – withdrawn."

"Ummm," the doctor paused, keeping his gaze on Benton as though he had been able to read Benton's thoughts and was awaiting more comments. Benton also waited. Finally as the silence between them deepened, the doctor cleared his throat. "You don't feel you can keep her in quarters, Mr. Benton?"

"I can keep her at home. I can get someone to be with her when I'm outside. I want to keep her at home." Benton wished the man to realize that *in quarters* was home, Martha's and his home. "However, is doing that the best thing for her? Doctor, she hasn't spoken a word in months, not to me, not to friends, not to the women who come in to care for her. She doesn't care if she's dirty, if she has clothes on. She sleeps endlessly; she cries sporadically, has periods where she gives these deep sighs, moans a little. Actually it's not moaning; it's more a keening, an eerie high-pitched long, drawn-out wail." Benton waved one hand in the air as if grasping for the right words. "That doesn't explain the sound accurately, but it's the best I can do."

"Yes, I've heard her." The psychiatrist thought Benton's description quite good. Martha Benton was not the only patient who wailed. It was a sound never to be forgotten, as though the individual had suffered a deep loss and the grief was tearing out the soul, as though the sound came from the very core of the being and was flung out in total despair. If it were due solely to tower living, why had it taken years to show up? Maybe it had merely been ignored earlier. So far in Babel-ON only a small number of people were classified as emotionally unstable, and a smaller number yet were institutionalized.

Of course, there had been in the early part of the twenty-first century, during the Time of Chaos, hordes of ill or unstable people in the population, both in the United States and around the industrialized world. With adequate care unavailable, many of the unstable had merely been ignored or had died of other illnesses resulting from the instability. At that time, treatment for even short-term curable illnesses had been in short supply, let alone treatment for long-term mental illness with its need for custodial care. Then, any deaths had been for the best. Even now, society would not be able to tolerate large numbers of non-functioning citizens. Of course, exceptions could be made for "special" cases. The fact that Martha Benton was the daughter-in-law of the late George Stokes Benton insured that every effort would be made on her behalf to keep her comfortable and to try and restore mental stability.

"Let's try more intensive therapy," the doctor concluded. "I promise, Mr. Benton, we'll do our best."

As Benton stood outside the door of Martha's cubicle, he thought about the many times he had visited her. He sighed. Visited was not the right word. He came and sat with her, but seldom did Martha give any indication of his presence. Twice over the years he recalled that she briefly had seemed some better.

"Amos! I'm so glad you're here," Martha had greeted him on a visit three years previously. For several weeks she had been able to carry on a lucid conversation, and both he and the psychiatrist had been guardedly hopeful. However, within a short period of time she was once more lost to him, back in some world of her own.

Again, Benton sighed but determinedly moved to Martha's beside. Partially propped up by two large pillows she lay with her eyes closed, breathing shallowly. "Martha, Martha, I'm here again," Benton softly called her name. "Can you hear me?"

Gradually her eyes opened but did not focus on anything nor did they move in his direction. Leaning over the bed, Benton began stoking her hair, pushing it back from her forehead. He noted that its once dark brown was nearly white and curled in wispy strands around the collar of her thin cotton gown. Fine lines were etched on her forehead as in a perpetual frown, and he tried to smooth them out.

"Martha, it's me. Amos. I'm here, Martha."

As he continued speaking, tears began to run down her cheeks, glistening rivulets against the pale, dry skin. There was no sound, just the tears oozing down her face and beginning to dampen her gown. Benton withdrew her hand from his, rang for an attendant and moved away toward a wall. He stared at the figure in the bed. Who was this woman? Could it be the same woman he had married, had loved? He tried to picture her as a bride, her breasts firm and tantalizing. After they made love, she always turned on her right side, her rear end tight against his groin. He would cup his hand around her breast, and they would settle into sleep. The memory was becoming ever fainter.

Slowly Martha moved her head and looked at him, or at least in his direction. The tears became sobs, accompanied by low moans. Benton realized that he did not know this woman – this stranger – and could not help her. Whatever was hurting her now was such that he could not understand. Apparently something within her mind, some memory, was too much for her to tolerate. The sound was heart-rending, was frightening, was as final as he had always imagined death would be. He knew then, in those few moments, that Martha Benton would not recover, was gone from him forever.

Automatically he helped the attendant hold her and watched as a needle pierced her arm. He dried her eyes, again pushed the damp hair away from her face and neck and talked softly to calm her. Just before Martha slept, Benton said his goodbye and left the room as he had entered it, to the sounds of her light breathing.

Once out of the Custodial Care Center, Benton headed for a large bank of elevators. He would concentrate only on his work, and his major mission now was to make sure the supplies were being readied for his and Shaner's trip outside. A thought suddenly flashed in his head. Had Martha found her own way to leave the tower – to get outside?

Chapter Six

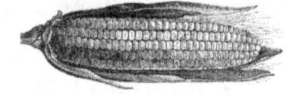

*A*s the darkness gave way to half-light, Solomon John pushed aside the report he had been studying. Although he had worked through the night, he did not feel that he had accomplished much. He felt uneasy, anticipatory. Actually he wasn't sure of his feelings. Since his conversation with Benton the previous evening, something had been hovering in the back of his consciousness – a premonition of trouble.

John turned to the window behind his desk and peered into the golden haze that shimmered in the sunrise. He was fortunate to have an office with an exterior outlet. Most living and working facilities in Babel-ON were illuminated artificially with the "second sun." Between the artificial light and the second sun, the tower's interior could take on the glow of midmorning or a hazy winter afternoon. Still, the warmth was lacking, and John could faintly recall the heat of a July sun on sizzling asphalt. His nose wrinkled involuntarily as he hurriedly shook his head. Rarely did he think of pre-tower times, and he resolved now to stop entirely. He, of all people, thoroughly supported the concept of tower living. Tower living was synonymous with human survival.

Awkwardly John rubbed at the glass pane but soon realized that the combination of its thickness plus years of crusty grime on its exterior would permit only a limited view of the countryside. As the day took hold, he thought he could make out the spot where fields met the horizon but wasn't sure. From the height of his office, the fields of grain seemed totally flat, with narrow ribbons of gray roads bordering celadon patches which faded into the distance to become sky.

*Non-sustainers in those fields? This close to Babel-ON? How could that be permitted? It **would not** be permitted!* He shook his head to emphasize the thoughts. It had taken nearly fifty years to reach the present level of tower living, and only the last fifteen years had been relatively free of suicides and civil unrest. True, there were still many parts of the globe where people continued to live outside towers, but individuals no longer owned land as their forefathers had. Today, it was the "old tower" countries of Europe, Canada, Australia and the United States, along with some parts of Brazil and China, which were supporting the starving millions in nations still too agriculturally disorganized to sustain their citizens. No one could be allowed to menace the present functioning system. If there were people outside, it was imperative that they be found and disciplined.

John stretched his six-foot frame toward the ceiling, hoping to stall a feeling of drowsiness that was becoming steadily more insistent. His thoughts returned to Benton. There was something about the man that John found disturbing, but he couldn't rationally explain why. He had felt this same way when George Stokes Benton had first introduced his son, the teenaged Amos. John had been so grateful to the senior Benton for selecting him from hundreds of other graduate architectural students for the position of junior architect and business manager of the tower project. Because of this initial selection, John had risen in influence in the tower hierarchy and now was known, to some degree, internationally. His present position was due mainly to that original push by George Stokes Benton. To repay his debt, John had tried to aid the son whenever he could. Although Amos Benton was only about nine years younger than Solomon John, the Bureau Manager always felt like a parent talking to a child, a superior directing a subordinate. Actually, John had to admit, they never really talked. He talked; Benton listened. John snorted, "Appears to listen is more like it. Tolerates what I say." John quickly looked around, aware that he had spoken aloud in the empty room.

Debt or not, there was something about the younger Benton that always caused him to be uncomfortable in the other's presence. John had a suspicion that Amos played the part expected of George Benton's son and heir, but that underneath that role was an unhappy and dissatisfied renegade of a man. Still, Benton performed his work in a more than satisfactory manner, and John realized that he really had no complaint with the man or his partner, Shaner.

And that brought his thoughts to Shaner. John recollected seeing the man's personnel file. William Karl Shaner, age twenty-six, born and reared in Babel-ON, the older of two brothers. An early convert to tower living, Shaner's father had been a dedicated employee of the Bureau of Sustenance but was killed during the days of Chaos. At first, Shaner's mother had some trouble adjusting to tower life but seemed stable enough now. Shaner was unmarried but involved with a dietician, Lana Howard from the Bureau of Nutriment Application, which controlled the quality and processing of all foodstuffs. Shaner appeared to be a bright young man, and he and Benton made a good team – prompt with reports, accurate in predictions of crop production, supportive of the sustainers. With over twenty years difference in their ages, Benton was closer to being a father to Shaner than a teammate, which could be helpful at times. However, it wasn't Shaner that prompted John's concern. It was something odd about Benton.

John shrugged as he heard his secretary enter the outer office. He needed to concentrate on the Bureau's immediate problem. "Good morning, Mrs. Crowley," he called. "Please get paperwork set up to send Benton and Shaner outside the tower for a week, possibly two."

Chapter Seven

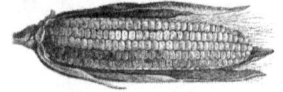

"All this doesn't bother you?" Shaner made a wide sweep with his hand as Benton steered their vehicle along the highway in the vicinity of what once had been Hannibal, Missouri. Coming to a junction, Benton decelerated slightly and headed more to the northwest toward the border of Iowa. He hoped this route 36 would be quicker than the one they had used previously, old highway 6 that was narrow and winding.

"All what bother me?"

"All this *nothing*." Shaner again waved his hand toward the expanse of fields and sky. "All this emptiness."

"I don't know what you mean by the word bother," Benton began cautiously, trying to formulate an answer that he felt would be safe.

"You know," Shaner's voice took on a slightly irritated tone. "The fact that there are no people, no one to help you if you need help, no, no . . . no noise even."

"Well, it is quiet. I'll give you that. But, no, I guess I've never thought about there being no one to help. There are sus-

tainers out in those fields most of the time during the growing season, but it's hard to see them now with the corn so tall.
If these were soy bean fields or onion plots, or just cattle pas-
ture, you'd be able to see sustainers working three to four
months of the year. They'd help you if you really needed it."

"Yeah, I guess so." Shaner let it rest for a minute. "You
lived outside a good while didn't you?"

"Yes, until I was in my early teens," Benton replied. Here
it was, the native-born distrust of those who had "immi-
grated" into the towers when all private property was about to
be confiscated for the greater good of all mankind. Or maybe
it wasn't distrust that he heard in Shaner's voice. Maybe it was
only simple curiosity. "Was there something particular that you
wanted to ask me about that time?"

"I don't know. I don't know if I know enough about it to
know what I want to know." They both laughed at Shaner's
round-about comment. "Did you live in a separate house? Was
it a big place?"

"Yes, I lived in a house with my parents – in Boulder,
Colorado – or at least I remember that house as a small boy. I
guess my parents were living there when I was born, but they
might have been in an apartment for a while. I don't think I
ever asked them." Benton slowed the truck for a moment as
they approached an old signpost and then accelerated.

"My father was a professor at the university there in
Boulder. Course nearly all of Colorado is in the Denver
tower now." Benton had Shaner's rapt attention. "And, yes, I
guess it was a big house. It was old, like the old woman's
house, only with larger rooms and high ceilings – about ten
rooms, as I recall. I remember as the winters seemed to grow
longer and harsher, my mother complained about the place

being too hard to heat, and my father grumbled about the cost of gas."

"Gas? Gasoline?" Shaner interrupted.

"No, natural gas. A great many houses were heated with natural gas."

"Didn't you have solar?"

"No, we didn't, although many homes around us – the newer ones – utilized a great deal of passive solar energy. Our home had been in mother's family since the late 1880s, and it was very fashionable then to remodel big older homes. I remember how spacious it was, how I could go off upstairs and be busy by myself for hours."

Benton stopped speaking. He could almost feel the solitude, the privacy, the sense of well-being, knowing someone was in the house but apart, knowing the feeling of pride of ownership, knowing the feeling of permanence. *How could he still feel so strongly after years in Babel-ON? How could he allow himself to yearn so strongly for the old ways? It was unhealthy. The towers were all there were. The towers had saved humanity. His father had saved humanity by his foresight to design them. "Tower Teamwork," the slogan had been in the chaotic times of early tower living. Now the experiment born out of necessity had succeeded. "Tower Triumphant" the new slogan read – triumphant over famine and fear. But at what cost?*

"Uh, you were saying," Shaner prodded, interrupting Benton's contemplation. "Wasn't it scary being off by yourself?"

Benton laughed. "Not really." He would have to be more cautious. Those spells of reverie in public were not good. "Used to go hunting and fishing by myself; a lot of people did. Course, as you know, with the size of the population it was difficult to be almost any place totally alone, except in your own home." He broke off suddenly. "Look! Look, Bill, a raccoon, I think. There along side that fence." Benton slowed the vehicle, as the animal scampered into the brush. "Odd that it would be out so boldly in broad daylight." At one time seeing wild animals was rare as they had been eliminated in droves to prevent them from raiding sustainer fields for food.

"Well, it probably feels secure now that the old ban on poisoning wildlife has been put into force. Still, wild animals can do a lot of damage to crops, cause a lot of lost bushels, couldn't they? I don't understand the latest edict on wildlife preservation at the expense of human food." Shaner rolled his window up as the raccoon scampered into the corn rows. "Seems to me those animals could add to the food supply, if you ask me."

"You may have just solved our problem for us, Bill," Benton began as the truck again picked up speed. "Think about the corn which has been missing from the old women's acreage. No person could stay alive on corn alone. Whoever he is, he must be living off some wildlife, raccoons, rabbits, squirrels, maybe even an occasional deer. You'd think someone would have reported seeing bones somewhere around, wouldn't you?"

"Would it be that easy to catch or hunt an animal? Wouldn't he need a gun? You said you had hunted once. What's it like?"

Momentarily Benton was stumped. His partner was continually asking him questions, and it often was like trying to explain something to a small child. Shaner would want a complete description of hunting, with all of its ramifications, in a few minutes of conversation. Still, his partner always seemed

interested and listened intently to answers that Benton sup-
plied to any of the young man's questions.

"No, it wouldn't be necessarily easy to hunt, and, no, a
gun wouldn't have to be used – to answer two of your questions. He could use a bow and arrows or maybe traps, if he was
smart enough to make them. Course both of those methods
would take skill and practice. Guess if he'd been outside for
some time he'd have time to practice though. And I don't
know if I can adequately describe hunting to you."

Benton glanced briefly at his watch. "Only ten o'clock. With
a little luck we can be at the old woman's shortly after noon." The
road was good, and Benton increased the speed a little as he
mulled over how to continue answering Shaner's questions.

"To begin with, usually only my dad and I went hunting.
Mostly we went in the autumn months, November, as I recall
and before the winters became so deadly. My grandfather on
my mother's side used to have a big ranch out east of Boulder
on the high plains as they were called. He and my grandmother didn't survive Chaos."

Benton paused, trying to see the two old people in his
mind. "At any rate I can almost picture the endless khaki of the
western fields bordered in spots by crusty snow which through
a process of melting and refreezing had lost its whiteness and
had become a sort of frothy cream color. On one hunt I recall
that tumbleweeds were piled high against the fences, and the
wind blew skiffs of new snow into gullies and around the few
flat rocks scattered here and there. We had been going rabbit
hunting, but somehow we ran into a few antelope – not a big
herd – just ten or twelve. My dad and I both took a shot, and
one of us got one. I don't think we ever ate him. Actually, I
can't remember for sure what we did with him. But it was

exciting stalking the game and being out so far from the city. Summers we would go fishing for trout or anything else that we could catch. We usually ate all of the fish we caught or cleaned them and gave them to friends. Everyone loved trout."

"I don't know." Shaner was silent for a few minutes. "I can't imagine eating a real piece of fish instead of a processed wafer made of one. I guess I just can't seem to feel what you're telling me."

"Well, I'm not sure it made too much sense even back in those days when we did it. Dad hunted; dad's dad hunted, and I guess I just took it for granted that I would go hunting, too."

"Somehow I can't imagine George Stokes Benton living outside," Shaner ended lamely. "I guess since the tower was his brainchild, I assumed he would have always lived a life similar to tower living."

"Oh, he certainly believed in tower living as the only survivable way for humans in the future. Of course, mother and I did, too," Benton added hastily.

Shaner looked at him for a minute, but Benton did not take his eyes off the road. "And, Martha? You met Martha in the tower?"

"Yes, Martha was only four when her parents opted for tower living. Of course, they and she went through part of Chaos, but she was too young to remember much about that ghastly time and really liked to be in a tower."

Benton wondered if that last statement was a true one, but he wanted to get off the subject of Martha. "How about you and Lana. How did you two meet, and should I begin looking for a wedding gift?" He laughed and looked at Shaner.

"Lana and I met because of friends. I'm in love with her, I think. Or I guess I am. But I don't know about a wedding –

not anyways soon. We're both old enough and I think she would like to get married. I guess she's the right woman for me, but how would I know? How did you know Martha was the woman for you?"

You had to hand it to Shaner Benton thought. *He could ask questions, particularly ones that you didn't wish to answer or couldn't answer. However, I guess this means that he is finally getting comfortable with me as his partner.*

"I don't know, Bill, not exactly. I just saw her – met her –at a required event, and we got to talking. I liked her looks, and I liked what she said. I sort of felt she might be the woman for me. I guess the fact that she seemed to like me, too, didn't hurt." Benton again glanced at his watch and to distract Shaner said, "Look at those fields. It's going to be a bumper crop this year.'

"I guess so," Shaner responded and then asked, "What if it weren't a bumper crop? What if something happened to the corn and other food? What would we do? What would the rest of the world do?"

"Well, rest easy. The harvest **will be** a good one," Benton reassured Shaner. "And if there is a bad year, one where the crops are smaller than anticipated or where the weather turns bad and some of the crops can't be fully harvested, there are stores of grain all over the country and in other countries, too."

"I guess so," Shaner replied, but he still seemed uncertain. "I guess you're right."

"Certainly am," Benton emphasized. "You're not gonna starve to death, and since we are making good time, we may get something special to eat from Mrs. Yates."

"Step on it. I can taste that corn now," Shaner said.

As Benton pressed down on the accelerator, he glanced at his partner and saw that Shaner had a big smile on his face.

Chapter Eight

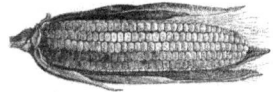

During the week after the two Bureau men previously had left the fields, Margot and Michael had been up late at night trying to anticipate what any return visit might lead to.

"Are you certain this is a good move, Margot? To try and capture them when – or if they come back?" He spoke quietly so as not to disturb the others.

"Michael, I'm not sure of anything. Not anymore." She paused and wiped her hand across her forehead, brushing a stray strand of hair from her eyes. "No, that's not true. I'm sure if we don't do something drastic now, this next spring we'll all be dead of starvation or its effects within two years. Maybe even less than two years. You can see that, can't you?"

Yes, he could see that. He could see it just by looking at his older sister, her body pitifully thin. She had taken over when the parents and all of the older boys and girls had died in the accident, when he had been only about the age Jamie was now. Anna, their cousin, was older than Margot and should have become the leader as the eldest survivor. However, the loss of her parents and both of her older brothers had left her in a state of semi-shock. Bewildered was the name Margot had given to Anna's acceptance of whatever happened, her inability to assume any responsibility, her sitting quietly hour by hour mumbling to herself. "She's just bewildered; she'll be better soon," Margot kept repeating over the months, but Anna was as she had been ever since the catastrophe.

"Yes, I can see what you're saying is true, Margot. I just hope we're capable of capturing the men without getting caught ourselves. But, when we've got them, then what?"

"I don't know yet, Michael," Margot replied in an exasperated tone. "I won't know until the time comes. We've got to leave here, and we need help to do it. I'm hoping that if we keep them with us all winter, we can convince them to help. If we can get them interested in one of the girls . . ."

"One of the girls," Michael broke in. "One? How about two or three of the girls?" He laughed.

"I don't think it's all that funny." She snapped at him. "If you think they will let Robin have you all to herself forever, you had better think again. We have Jamie for the younger girls, Margaret, Connie and Beth. But without other men, the clan won't be able to grow in size. Noreen, Lauren and Lucille will have to remain childless — even the younger girls"

"Not to mention you," Michael interjected, noting that Anna had not been included in the group of females.

"Yes, that's true, of course. But I wasn't thinking of myself. What's worse, Michael, is that we have to be so careful of who mates with whom. The elders always said it would be bad enough that most of us are distant cousins, but brother and sister mating . . ." She let the thought hang. "Well, we will have to try to do something, that's all."

"Remember, the elders had it all planned out, which male and which female belonged together. Didn't they have you paired with Matthew?"

"Yes, I guess they did." Margot knew Michael was correct, but she would rather have forgotten the matter. Because of the close genetic backgrounds, mating was planned on the basis of necessity not attraction. Actually she had not liked Matthew as well as she had liked her cousin Kenneth, but Kenneth was programmed to marry Matthew's sister. When they had planned the haven, the elders had assumed that they and any future offspring would be there only a limited number of years and would then be able to emerge and set up some sort of communal lifestyle far away from any tower. She remembered as she was growing up the nights of talking about what life would be like once they left the haven. However, the old ones had not been able to foresee the extent of the changing world nor the necessity of tower living. As one year followed another, they had still made plans to leave the haven eventually, but the physical development of the older children and the necessity to remain hidden longer had necessitated mating plans. Then the accident had changed everything.

"At any rate, Michael, you and Jamie may have to think of more than one wife, if that's the correct term anymore."

"Maybe not, if your plan works." He could remember Noreen's eyes on him at dinner the past night. He could also remember the nasty way Noreen now spoke to Robin and the suggestions she made about Michael being able to visit her when Robin "got too big." He thought of Connie who would soon be entering her teens and Anna, already thirty-three but with the mind of a child. He had selected Robin out of the group and was happy with her. "For now," Michael emphasized, "let's just concentrate on making your plan work."

"All right, then. We'll need to explain the plan to the others within the next few days. We also need to get as much corn stored as we can find so that we don't have to use what little food is still left from before the accident. Let's move out at night into some of the nearby fields and strip as many ears of corn as we can and dry it. Also if any berries remain that haven't been eaten by the wildlife, gather them. That may be our entire food supply soon. Then, regardless of which two men the Bureau sends back, we'll be ready for them."

"So you see what we're up against," Margot stopped talking and looked at each of the others gathered around her. Noreen, Lauren and Lucille nodded slightly, but there was no response of any kind from Anna. Robin looked quickly at Michael who tried to give her a reassuring smile. Connie, who at age nine was still considered one of the children, had been permitted to attend the discussion due to its serious nature, moved closer to Robin and took her sister's hand. Jamie now understood why Michael and Margot always appeared worried. Although he was proud to be considered old enough to be included in most group discussions, he began to wish that he had not "grown up" so fast. The youngest children, Beth and Margaret, had not been included and were, he knew, peacefully asleep.

"So you see," Margot repeated. "We can't stay here any longer, and, yet we can't really leave – not without some help at least. The plan I outlined earlier is the best solution that Michael or I could come up with."

"What makes you think your plan will work?" Noreen questioned impatiently. She was not fond of Margot nor did she like having the woman make most of the decisions about the group. Right now she resented not having been told at an earlier time about the crisis they were all facing. In addition she attributed Michael's liaison with Robin directly to Margot. At one time he had seemed to be attracted to her, but Margot had discouraged any sexual activity until all of them had recovered from the shock of the accident. Shortly thereafter Michael had become interested in Robin, who had discovered she was pregnant. Noreen's pale gray eyes fastened on the other woman, and in a few seconds Robin nervously turned to look at her. "Have you already made the final decision, Margot," Noreen continued, "or can some other input be made."

"By all means, Noreen. If you have something to contribute, please say so." Margot was determined not to let Noreen upset her at this critical moment when she was attempting to get each one to focus upon the seriousness of their situation.

"How much food is left?" Noreen decided that she needed some more information before making any suggestions.

"Very little of the original food from the old ones, " Michael answered before Margot could get her thoughts together. He could see that Noreen was set to bait Margot if she could. He could also see by the way her eyes flashed as she turned to him that she had not forgiven him for abandoning her in favor of Robin. Probably she dislikes Jamie, too, just because Margot and I are his brother and sister.

While he was no longer sexually aroused by Noreen, he could still recognize the beauty that had attracted him in the first place. The fair skin and silky blonde hair created an illusion of some nebulous night creature, a moon goddess perhaps, cool and transparent. Thinly disguised, however, were a coarse sensuality and a tendency toward possessiveness that had disturbed him. Still, as Margot had pointed out to him, at the present time he was the only surviving "man" among all of these young women.

"I'm sure you wondered, Noreen, why we were all scurrying around these past few nights, even several miles from the haven, gathering corn," Michael continued. "We need to dry as much corn as we can for it will be almost our only food for the coming cold months." He let them all think on this for several moments before continuing. "We'll harvest what we can of the current crop, if it doesn't freeze on the stalks before ripening, and Jamie has managed to bring in a fair supply of black walnuts. Of course, when the sustainers return to their tower, we can take what's left in the old woman's garden, but that will be mostly scraps of food — carrots and turnips, maybe a stray potato.

"Ugh!" Noreen responded. Turning her eyes on Robin again, she asked. "What about the new baby we're all expecting?" She emphasized the word "all" while looking around the room at each person. "It can't be expected to eat carrots and turnips, can it?"

Her mouth looks so ugly when she is trying to be snide Margot thought but continued smiling at the girl. "That's a good point, Noreen. We hope Robin will be able to nurse the baby; otherwise it will have to survive on what's left of the powdered milk."

Noreen had asked a very good question, Margot knew. Leave it to good old Noreen to go right to the heart of the problem and make you squirm if she could. It had been seven years since there had been a baby in the haven. Beth had been only five months old when the accident occurred. Fortunately the older girls had helped rear the younger children, and they had taken over mothering Beth who dutifully had drunk powdered milk and thrived. Now, Margot wondered, if they would be able to safely deliver a baby since none of them had any firsthand knowledge of the birth process. Babies being born had always been handily taken care of by the elders.

"The real problem," Michael continued as if he were still discussing the issue of the food supply, "is whether or not we have and can keep adequate amounts of food to take with us when we have to leave here."

"Oh, do we have to leave, Michael? Margot?" Connie begged, glancing anxiously from one to the other.

Margot could see the same question in the eyes of the others. "If you can come up with something better, let me hear it. As Michael outlined, we will be more undernourished this winter than last. You do remember last winter, don't you? We can eat up what little bit of original food is left – probably in under five months – and then what? We can't go outside during the day except for very brief periods of time for fear of being seen by sustainers. We can glean at night, but even then we can't take enough food to do much more than feed us each day. Plus it's not the right kind of food. We are getting almost no protein; we can't trap only in a very limited area for fear the traps will be found; we can't fish except just sporadically, and we have to put ourselves in jeopardy whenever we go down to the stream. Also, Michael is the only one who knows even a little bit about trapping and fishing " She stopped speaking momentarily and then said, "I suppose we could just eat everything up this last winter and then surrender ourselves to the Bureau."

"Oh, no!" They all chorused.

"Oh, Margot, not the tower," both Lucille and Lauren exclaimed in unison.

"Definitely not the tower," Michael echoed. "Besides, how do we know they would welcome us. We've had plenty of time to become towerites before now."

"True, Michael, although I don't think they'd do anything to us if we just suddenly showed up and asked to be let in. Still you never know," Margot ended lamely. "Well, if we aren't going to the tower, what are we going to do – other than what Michael and I are suggesting?"

"How do you know the Bureau men will want to help us, Margot?"

"They won't, Noreen," Margot said again turning to face her adversary. "That's why, as I indicated earlier, we will have to catch them, be really nice to them, keep them here with us until we can persuade them to be on our side." She did not add that she would be counting heavily on Noreen to do a great deal of the persuading.

"What if they don't ever get on our side," Lauren asked. "They'll know where we are living – hiding. We just can't let them go, can we?"

"I don't know, Lauren," Margot answered wearily. "We just can't predict everything. We, Michael and I, hope they will eventually be willing to help us."

"If not," Noreen slowly spaced each word, "we may have to kill them."

"Oh, Noreen," Margot chided, but the thought had apparently been in everyone's mind. *What would we do* Margot wondered thoughtfully. She looked at Noreen and shivered slightly. "At any rate, Jamie reports that the Bureau men are back – the same two that were here about a week ago, he thinks. Before we spend too much time worrying about what we will do with them, first we have to catch them."

When the others had left the discussion and were getting settled for the night, Margot crept outside the haven. Carefully she made her way to the old woman's house. All was dark and quiet. Apparently they were all asleep. After Jamie had said the men were back, Michael had gone at dusk to the house and had finally been able to get close enough to overhear snatches of conversation. The men were going to begin hunting for the corn culprits in the morning, so she must make sure that no one went outside the haven. When they had scoured the fields in daylight and had found nothing, she knew they would move into the trees and the ravines. Then, when they found nothing again, they would begin a search at night. Give them several days, she thought. Maybe when they find nothing, they will become complacent and relax their guard.

She moved back nearer the safety of the haven and paused to look at the night sky. The clear, crisp night made the stars appear very near. The moon was up, a quarter moon, which faintly outlined the trees, most of them already nearly bare of leaves. A few more days of late August, and the endless hours of the new winter would be upon them. What could they do? They couldn't stay here indefinitely but had to try and go somewhere away from the sustainers and towers. She remembered overhearing the elders discussing the possibility of moving to the northwest, along the old Canadian/American border. Apparently, they had heard rumors of others who had been able to avoid the towers by huddling in those more remote areas. Of course, that was years ago. Were there any other non-towerites now? If they could get to a more distant area, a much warmer place, she felt they could hide well enough that they could grow some food during the summer months which she hoped would be somewhat longer in weeks than where they were now. However, the big plus would be that they could hunt, trap and fish – a food supply that they were virtually denied now.

Jamie had said that the men had carried guns. *Why?* She mulled the idea of the guns over in her mind. *Were the guns merely for their protection? Protection from what? Other than a coyote or maybe a bear, there was little for them to fear. They must be expecting to encounter some danger. Are we the danger? Would the two men really shoot anyone found outside a tower?*

She thought of Noreen's comment about killing the Bureau men if they refused to adjust to the haven and then move with the others when the time came. Could she do that? Could she actually shoot someone? Of course, she was the leader; she couldn't expect the others to do what she would not do herself.

"Oh, well. We may just have to kill them," she said softly.

Chapter Nine

*W*hen Benton and Shaner entered the kitchen the morning after leaving Babel-ON, the old woman had breakfast prepared and already was eating her portion. "You two lay-a-beds would never make sustainers," was her greeting to them. "It's nearly six o'clock."

Both men laughed as they dished up plates of egg wafer and took pieces of bread which had been left over from the previous evening's meal. In a brown bowl on the table were small wedges of crab apples from three trees by the privy. Shaner cautiously tasted a piece and then helped himself to another. The old woman looked pleased.

"I made sure I got all the worms out," Mrs. Yates pointed to the apple slices. "Ain't too many apples left on that tree; birds and squirrels probably got most, but a couple of those on the ground are still fair for eatin'. Used to make tasty crabapple jelly way back, but now even if I had enough sugar out here, I doubt I'd ever get it to jell."

"Everything's fine, Mrs. Yates." Shaner smiled at her. "Egg wafers are fixed nicely."

"Used to have real eggs before the towers. Had a big chicken coop and got all the eggs we wanted. I used to make big angel food cakes for my father. Put twelve or fourteen eggs in a cake at one time. Lord, what I wouldn't give for a slice of angel food cake or a real fried egg, fried in bacon grease with the edges all crisp and the yolk just slightly runny."

"Yuk! Wouldn't that be awfully messy, an egg that wasn't cooked?" The only eggs Shaner had ever eaten were wafer eggs, usually cooked so that they were well-done. He remembered checking out a few years before an egg sustenance center which processed the raw eggs into wafers. While he was there, two eggs feeding into the processor had fallen from the conveyer belt and cracked open on the floor. He could still see the opaque yellow yolk oozing through slimy jelly. Egg wafers contained a lemon yellow egg batter consisting of finely powdered egg and shell. No part of the eggs was wasted, and it provided a good source of protein for the towerites.

Mrs. Yates had been staring at Shaner for a few minutes. Finally she spoke. "I guess it would be messy to your way of thinking, young fella. It's the natural way though, the way the Provider intended. I don't suppose the hen thought of it as being messy. You seen chickens, haven't you?"

"Certainly, I've seen chickens," Shaner replied, a little huffily, although he didn't admit that he had seen them only once and only since he had joined the Bureau of Sustenance as a surveyor of food production. Actually, he had never seen a raccoon before yesterday, but he didn't mention that either.

"Wonder how many people there are alive today who haven't seen a chicken," Benton asked conversationally. He had never considered the matter before but was suddenly intrigued by his own question. Unless someone visited a tower zoo, and many towers were not large enough to have all of the amenities of Babel-ON or the other massive population towers, he could live his entire life without seeing almost any animal except in a book or on television. There were, of course, pets in the towers, but these were exclusively birds or fish. Dogs and cats had been excluded right from the beginning as they consumed too much food otherwise needed for humans. The concerted government effort to cut down on the dog and cat population had led to them becoming almost extinct. During the days before his family had opted for tower living, Benton had two dogs, and he remembered the joy they had brought to him. He glanced at Shaner, thinking how sad it was that the young man had never known, would never know, the love that a dog could give to its owner. "Probably a lot of people seldom see any animal unless it's a mouse or rat," Benton added. Somehow even the invincible utopian tower had been unable to rid itself of those two pests.

"Well, who's got time to go to a zoo or fool around with animals anyway," Shaner added. Most people are probably too busy for that."

The old woman only grunted and began to clear away the dishes. "I'll just stack them now. Have plenty of time to do them tonight when it's too dark to be in the fields. Won't be back as early as last evening. Just came early then to see that you fellas were taken care of." She picked up an old hat, jammed it securely on her head and went out the door. Benton and Shaner followed her out.

"Be careful," she called as she headed away from them toward one of the fields.

"What do you think," Shaner began. They had been steadily combing the fields for over three hours without a break, looking for anything that would tell them more than they already knew. "There doesn't seem to be any footprints, just corncobs. And not a whole lot more of them than when we were here last week."

"I don't know what to think," Benton conceded. "I guess they could brush away their footprints as the ground is pretty hard. Hasn't been any rain for quite a spell now." He rubbed his forehead. "Some of these corncobs we've seen have just recently been cleaned though – maybe not last night but the night before at least."

"Then they're still out there, wherever *there* is?"

"It would seem so," Benton replied, "but I don't think they're anywhere in this particular field. Possibly in one of the nearby fields, although they could be miles away, eating a little bit or taking a little bit out of each field, and only the old woman was concerned enough to report them."

"Why would she be concerned if the other sustainers weren't," Shaner looked puzzled. "Would they be eating more from this cornfield than from the others? Would this corn be any better?"

"Got me," Benton shrugged. "I wouldn't think there'd be any difference in the corn from field to field. There shouldn't be." He paused for a few minutes as they pushed their way through a final barrier of stalks and came out on the path which led to the sump. "The garden," he said.

"The garden? What garden?"

"The old woman's garden – by her house. I thought when we were here before that they might be raiding a garden as I found some empty pea pods by the sump, along with all the corncobs. Since hers is the only house for miles around being used by a sustainer, it's the only garden for miles. I'll bet they come here more often, or at least regularly, to steal something additional from the garden."

"Sort of a little treat," Shaner laughed.

"Yes. You remember this morning. Mrs. Yates explained that there were not many apples left on the tree in her yard. Wonder if some of those apples disappeared not due to squirrels but into the stomachs of the same people who've been dining these past weeks on fresh corn."

"I suppose it could be," Shaner hesitated a minute to see if Benton was going to climb the small rise to the sump. When Benton did, Shaner followed. "But wouldn't you think she'd hear someone if they were stealing food out of her garden and off her apple tree?"

"You'd think so," Benton agreed. "Still . . ." He stopped as they reached the top of the mound and saw the sump again spread out before them. Even Shaner was silent. The midmorning sun glittered on the rippling water, causing them both to squint. Day-lilies which had been so perky just a few days earlier were now blooming sparsely, and their leaves were tinged with brown. *They know it's not long now* Benton thought. *Just these last few cool nights are making a big difference in all of the foliage.* Near one of the cottonwood trees, a small clump of sumac was beginning to turn scarlet, like a spot of blood on the hillside.

"Wonder if you could swim in there?" Shaner mused.

"Probably could, Bill, although I imagine it would be pretty cold right now. However, in midsummer a dip in the sump would probably be very refreshing. Course it may not be as deep as it looks, at least close to the far bank where you see all that scum on the surface of the water. You might get stuck in the mud over there."

"It's pretty in a lonely sort of way," Shaner admitted. "I can see why they come up here to eat their corn."

"My God," Benton began, "is that the world's foremost towerite I hear talking?"

Shaner laughed. "I didn't say I wanted to eat by it. I just said I could see that it had its own sort of beauty. That doesn't mean that I'd give up one day of the tower to be out here in this wild place. It still gives me the creeps – especially when it gets dark."

"Well, let's go on a little farther," Benton changed the subject. "Then we'll stop for lunch, or do you need a break now?"

"I can outlast you any day," Shaner replied good-naturedly.

They moved down to the end of the sump and dropped back into the corn field. About an hour later, after a quick lunch of mostly dried, vitamin-fortified fruit, they began searching the neighboring field to the north. When they finally returned to the house just as the sun was painting the sky a pale salmon color, they saw that the old woman was again in the kitchen.

"What'd you find?" Mrs. Yates asked as they dragged themselves through the door.

"Nothing!" Benton replied. "We walked miles today, looking everywhere we could think to look. And nothing! If there were someone out there today, he must be invisible."

The next few days took on the same pattern. Early each morning the two men would begin their scouting and steadily widened the circle until they had checked out most of the surrounding fields. Each evening when they returned to the old woman's house, they would report to her that there had been no sighting of any non-sustainer and spend a few pleasant hours eating and in conversation. Shaner seemed to have an endless number of questions, which both Mrs. Yates and Benton attempted to answer.

"Just how old are you, Mrs. Yates?" he abruptly asked one evening as they sat over steaming mugs of black tea.

"Now you know that's not a nice question to put to a lady," she chided him. "I'll tell you one thing though; I'll never see sixty again." She glanced over at Benton and met his eyes. "Well, matter of fact, I'll never see seventy again either." She chuckled and Benton laughed with her.

Shaner appeared stunned. He wasn't certain that he had ever talked with anyone who was past seventy years old. Of course, there were a few people that age in Babel-ON, but he could not remember ever speaking with them. He remembered vaguely his grandmother − his father's mother − had died at the age of sixty-eight, when he was only four years old. However, he recalled that she had been feeble, not hearty like Mrs. Yates. He knew that the Director of the Bureau was an old man, and he realized that most of the individuals in Congress and the President had lived a portion of their lives before Chaos. Still, seventy years seemed an impossible figure to him as most of the towerites with whom he came in contact were fairly young − certainly not in their seventies. Finally he spoke.

"Seventy years! I find that hard to believe. I guess I just didn't figure you were that old. I guess I didn't think you'd still be working. I guess . . . I don't know what I thought," he stammered a little. "I thought, well, I guess I thought that at. . . seventy. . . you'd be ready. . . " He looked at Benton for help, but Benton was enjoying the turn the conversation had taken and did not come to his aid.

"To die! Is that what you thought?" The told woman shot back at him. "Well, let me tell you something, Mr. Shaner (for days now he had been "young man" whenever she had addressed him), I forgot more about farmin' or sustaining as you all call it now than most of these young sustainers know. Oh, I'm aware that there's all this huge modern machinery and modern seed that ripens much faster than seed used to. But, there's seed and there's seed. I'm not certain this new seed has all the food value of the old days or that it is good for people. Nature's changing, and I'm not certain the way we're living now is the right way to meet these changes." She stopped suddenly, and Benton was glad she had before she said something that she might have regretted later. Shaner sat with his head lowered, like a student chastised by a teacher.

"He didn't mean any offense, Mrs. Yates." Benton spoke hurriedly to keep the silence from becoming overlong. "Bill was born in Babel-ON and has hardly ever – actually never – been outside except infrequently on Bureau business."

"Yes, I'm real sorry if I said anything I shouldn't have," Shaner added quickly.

"No harm done." Mrs. Yates took a sip of her tea. "I shouldn't get so riled up – not good for me at my age. I mean it. No offense taken, young man. Just having you to talk to is a real treat for me." She reached over and patted Shaner's hand. *By God* Benton thought. *He's charmed the old woman.*

After that episode Benton thought that Shaner might give up his questioning, but that was not to be. "Even though I can't picture you ever being a young girl, Mrs. Yates," he began several evenings later, "did you do a lot of different things for entertainment?" Benton could not believe the question had been put so clumsily, but the old woman seemed to take no notice this time.

Gazing off into space for a few minutes, she finally said, "Yes, I did an awful lot of things, or rather we did. We all went to a county school where most everyone knew everyone else. We went to parties and dances, football games, picnics." She stopped momentarily. "Matter of fact, we used to have a picnic ever now and then up by the sump, just like the ones that are stealing my corn."

Shaner digested this bit of information in silence, so she continued. "I got my first car right after I was sixteen. Daddy got it for me so I could go places without having to pester mother and him. It was a bright red Chevrolet." She looked triumphantly at Shaner. He nodded, although he had no idea what a Chevrolet was. He considered interrupting her to ask for an explanation but decided he would wait and get an answer from Benton later that evening when they all retired.

"I remember we used to drive clear into Kansas City just to get a Coke, and sometimes we even went as far as Des Moines just for the thrill of driving," Mrs. Yates continued. "Course, mother, daddy and I went to Kansas City or St. Louis several times a year, too. All those towns are gone now . . . all those houses . . . all the people . . . just nothing left but the fields." She shook her head. "Well, as I was saying we had dances, and I loved to dance. I remember mother and I went to Kansas City to look for a dress for the senior dance. It was such a pretty dress, pink. Those were the good old days, the earlier part of the century. Well," she corrected herself, "Maybe not so good for some. There were some getting killed in the wars in Africa. The whole country was upset over them. You know about the wars, don't you?" Again she looked directly at Shaner.

"Uh, yes," he responded quickly. Actually he could only faintly remember some mention of it in a college history class, but he didn't want to get into a discussion of past wars. There had not been a war for over thirty years, unless, of course, one considered the rioting and killing during Chaos.

"Well, at any rate, that dance was where I met my husband, Roger." She paused again, lost in reminiscence.

"Had you known him before?" Benton finally spoke up.

"Oh, I'd seen him before, if that's what you mean. But I hadn't known him. Come to think of it, I never did know him." She took another sip of tea. "We got married soon after I got out of high school. Then the baby came and then he left." She got up from her chair and brought the hot water from the stove, adding it to the few tea leaves still in the pot. After refilling all three cups, she asked, "What's your plan for tomorrow? Where you plan to look now?"

Story time is over Benton thought and realized that she had never before mentioned having had a child. "I don't think we're going to do any looking tomorrow, Mrs. Yates. I think Bill and I will just stay around your house, rest and sleep if we can, and then go out tomorrow night and see what we can see. Can't find anything in the day, but maybe we will be luckier when it's dark."

"If that's the case, I'm wondering if one of you could drive me back to the sub-tower. Know it's about a fair drive one way, but if we left early, you could still be back by noon and have time to nap. It wouldn't do you no good to get into the fields until way after dark. Someone needs to take reports back on the progress with harvest in this area, and I can do that as well as the next person."

"That'd be okay, wouldn't it?" Shaner asked.

"Don't see why not," Benton replied. "That will give me a chance to get a message to Solomon John so he'll know of our progress – or lack of progress – I guess I should say. Also let him know when we expect to return to Babel-ON."

He turned to Mrs. Yates. "Don't you get too worried if we aren't here when you come back as we may camp in the field for a night or two. I'm sure you can feel how much colder the nights have become just in the few days we've been here. So, if we don't find something within the next few days, we'll have to give up until next year. Wouldn't surprise me if we found a skiff of frost on the ground tomorrow morning or the day after."

A half hour later, all three were in bed, but Benton and Shaner were quietly discussing the short trip to the sustainer's tower and the next night's hunt. "I'm not sure I'm going to like camping out," Shaner complained. "I don't really like staying in this house. It's like camping out to me."

"Don't worry, Bill," Benton reassured him. "It won't be much different from this, except it will be colder and you won't get any hot water like Mrs. Yates fixes for us." Benton hoped Shaner wouldn't take the teasing the wrong way. When Shaner had grumbled about his quick morning shower in cold water, Mrs. Yates had prepared him a bath one day in her old bathroom, heating large containers of water on the kitchen stove. It was the first bath Shaner had ever had, and he liked it. In the towers, there were no tubs, only showers.

"I'll get even with you for that crack," Shaner laughed. "Seriously though, I'm sure I'll survive, but I'm not gonna like it."

"Think of Mrs. Yates. She enjoys living this way – in this house during the growing season – ever chance she gets. She's over seventy and she takes cold showers just like you and I have had to do."

"Yeh," Shaner agreed. "She's a gutsy old girl. Actually I've grown sort of fond of her, even if she's always sort of grumpy and always telling me off. You know, I think she sort of likes me, too." Shaner yawned, turned toward the wall and mumbled a "g'night."

Benton was amazed. A week out of Babel-ON and Shaner had allied himself with an old sustainer who kept muttering things that were only a little this side of treason. He caught himself just before he laughed aloud. He wasn't sure this change in Shaner was for the best, since they would be returning shortly to Babel-ON. He agreed that the old woman liked Shaner, had almost adopted him. As he settled more snugly in his sleeping bag, he thought he heard a rustling outside the window but decided it was too chilly to get up and check it out. He thought again of Shaner and the old woman. Benton also liked Bill Shaner, and he hoped that being with him and listening to both Mrs. Yates and himself would not in some way bring harm to his young colleague, especially if Shaner said something that Solomon John might judge to be anti-tower. He pulled the blanket higher around his neck and thought momentarily of the upcoming trip with the old woman. He would be able to drop her off at the sustainer station and be back with Shaner early the next afternoon.

Chapter Ten

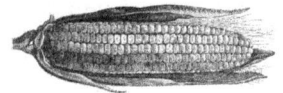

*J*amie was scared. As he crouched in the brush, his throat dry and constricted, a slight queasiness tugged at his stomach, and he felt the need to urinate. "Settle down; settle down," he whispered to himself. "Take deep breaths. It's fine. Everything will be fine. Settle down."

Slowly he began to relax and finally sat back, stretching his legs cautiously in front of him. He wiggled his toes vigorously to lessen the discomfort of a slight cramp in the calf of his left leg. It would be several minutes until sunset, and he had been instructed not to leave his hiding place until dusk. All the time his eyes had been following the two men.

The nights were growing colder, and he shivered slightly. He hoped the plan would work. It would work! Michael had assured him that nothing could go wrong if he did exactly as they had planned. Even Margot had been confident he could handle it, or maybe she had just wanted to boost his confidence in himself.

He shivered again. He was scared. If only they all weren't depending on him. If only there were another male, other than

Michael, older than him, but there wasn't. The other males were all long dead. Even now his lower lip trembled as he thought of his mother. He still missed her, still could remember the sound of her laughter, although he couldn't seem to recall her face any longer except in an occasional dream. When he was younger, Margot had done her best to ease the loss, but now that he was thirteen, he had asked to be treated more like an adult and to carry his share of the workload with Michael and the other women. Even Beth, age eight, was still thought of as a child and was somewhat indulged and pampered by all of them.

Dusk was now settling rapidly over the fields making it harder to see, and he rubbed at his blue eyes, being careful not to get dirt in them. A lock of his blonde hair, so light in color that it was almost white, lay across his forehead, and he pushed it back into place. Suddenly he became aware that he was not alone. A rabbit had appeared near him and had begun to nibble on a few shoots of dusty grass, apparently unaware of his presence. "Margot's always saying I can't sit still," he again whispered to himself, startling the rabbit which looked up but did not move away. Glancing back at the men, he could see that now they were coming toward him. A small glow of pride swept over him and he thought *Like you, Mr. Rabbit, they won't know I'm here until I want them to.*

Shaner and Benton had been searching in the fields all the previous night. In fact, this was their sixth day out of Babel-ON. Both men had driven the old woman to her sub-tower and had sent a message to Solomon John indicating that they would stay outside another week unless the weather prohibited it. At the end of that time, if they had not found anything significant, they would return and file a report to that effect.

"Probably see you before you leave for good," Mrs. Yates had told them. "I expect to get back out there in two, three days just to get things all checked out for the winter. Make yourselves at home like I said and use anything that's in the house that you need including the bit of firewood. Just don't get careless and burn the place down."

Now as the twilight waned and the woods became darker, Benton motioned in the direction of the house and said to Shaner, "Let's head back to the house if we don't find anything soon. Can't stand another night in the cold without being warm enough to get some sleep, Bill. Either nothing's out here or they're smarter than we are."

"Well, we're still finding corn cobs. Either they've come and gone or they're invisible."

"That could be – that they've been and gone," Benton agreed. "I don't see how they can be in this field or anywhere close by, unless they keep moving just ahead of us. I swear we've walked over every inch . . ."

"Maybe that's it," Shaner piped up suddenly. "Maybe they aren't in the fields except when they need to get food. Maybe there's another house like the old woman's, and they come here to throw us off the track. Maybe we've been too quick to discount that idea." Shaner had mentioned the idea before, but Benton had failed to react to it.

"That's still a thought, Bill." Benton stretched and shifted the rifle to his other shoulder. "Although if there is another house, it must be miles away or we'd have seen it, wouldn't we? We've even questioned all of the sustainers in the nearby fields. Wouldn't they have mentioned a house if there was one?"

"Suppose so. Still, I think we might consider the possibility. Might just be part of a torn-down building, not a real house."

"Well, we're not making any progress the way we're doing it now. That's for sure," Benton shrugged. "Okay, tomorrow we see if we can locate any part of another sustainer's old place. We'll drive north and east first."

He waved a hand toward the northeast, noting that there was a glimmer of lightening faint in the distance. *Hope it doesn't begin to rain before we get to the old woman's place* Benton thought. He knew that rain this late in the summer could often become hail and make those caught outside very uncomfortable. Birds were settling into nearby trees for the night, and the evening breeze was considerably more brisk than when the two of them had first come to the old woman's place nearly a week earlier. Benton shivered. If it could get this much colder so quickly, how many days did they have left for the search before they would be forced to return to Babel-ON. He turned up the collar of his coat and sniffed the air. "God, it smells good!" he exclaimed. "Even though it's cold, nothing will ever smell this good again."

Shaner gave a short laugh. "Actually it doesn't smell too bad, considering there's nothing out here but all this green stuff. But don't think I'm turning into a sustainer just 'cause I've got some dirt on my shoes." He turned to wait for Benton who had lagged behind. "Still, I never thought I'd eat raw food and wash now and then in cold water. If we don't get back to Babel-ON soon, I'll have become a savage."

"What do you mean a savage?" Benton picked up the bantering tone. "All of us lived like this – all of civilization – before you were even born, born into that specialized tower

hothouse. Course then we always had hot water for washing .
. ." Benton stopped abruptly, grabbing Shaner's shoulder.

"What's that, Bill? Over there in the scrub at the side of
the field. See? See it?"

"I see it! I see it!" Shaner's voice became louder. "It's
some animal. No, it'someone. Looks like a child. Where's he
going?" Shaner broke into a run with Benton at his heels.
"He's heading toward those trees over there." They had picked
up speed, trying to keep sight of the running figure.

"Damn, it's getting too dark," Benton panted as they
stumbled along the edge of the corn furrows. "If he gets to
that gully, we'll never find him again."

The men increased their speed, trying not to trip in the
dusk, trying to keep the individual in sight. The boy could hear
the sound of their boots scuffling across the dry earth. He
forced himself to slow down to make certain they could see
him. It was almost more than he could bear as his mind kept
insisting *Hurry! Hurry! Run! Run!*

Several days prior he had walked the trail which had
been made by deer, trying to foresee every rock or tree limb
that might be in his path; still the trail seemed unfamiliar. A
quick look over his shoulder confirmed that the two men
were gaining slightly. He forced his eyes to stay on the ground.
"Careful," he intoned. "Don't want to trip. Not too far now."

"I think he's tiring," Shaner yelled as they followed the
running figure into the trees. "Let's see if we can get him."

Benton was surprised at how awkwardly he and
Shaner were moving while the boy seemed as agile as an
animal. Sprinting was not a major part of the exercise programs required in Babel-On as merely running laps in a
gym could be extremely boring. Competitive games were

what encouraged participation and kept up interest in physical fitness. *Of course, how many times had the two of them had to run after someone since there was no place for anyone to run to. Now he knew there was a place to run to — outside! Somehow this boy had been living outside. How was that possible?* He couldn't get his thoughts to coincide with what he was seeing.

"We're gonna get him," Shaner panted. "We're closing in. Just a ..."

The ground seemed to give way beneath them, and they tumbled together, a jumble of arms and legs. Benton felt his boot gouge into soft flesh and heard a soft "Uhhh" from Shaner. As Benton fell, the butt of his rifle crashed against his nose. Blood began to ooze into his mouth, and the taste made him nauseous. Abruptly he and Shaner were jerked to a halt as figures surrounded and steadied them.

"It's a net ... a Goddam net," Shaner began as needles were jabbed into their arms. The night began to grow even blacker, and both men lapsed into semi-consciousness.

———————

"Jamie, get up that tree and untie the net," a woman's voice rang out. The boy quickly did as he was told. "Hurry, everyone! Bind their hands and feet. Come on! Hurry! There's a thunderstorm coming by the look of the sky. Before it hits we need to be in the haven so we don't leave any tracks."

Laboriously they began to half-carry, half-drag the two men toward the gully.

Chapter Eleven

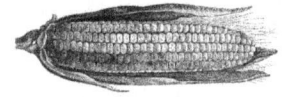

*B*enton opened his eyes to a tiny shaft of sunlight filtering through an opening which was covered with a tangle of vines and leaves. As his eyes focused more clearly, he could see it was a window but with glass so dirty that it provided a minimum of illumination. His mouth was dry and his head ached. *They must have beaten us* Benton thought, trying to remember the sequence of events before he had become unconscious.

"Bill, you there?" he called softly. There was no reply, but Benton knew he could hear someone breathing. He squinted, trying to penetrate the gloom. Something buzzed near his ear. He recognized the sound as a mosquito, although he seldom saw bugs, flies or other types of flying pests in Babel-ON. Occasionally a few made it into the tower when doors from the outside were opened for towerites' supplies to be unloaded and stored. As he struggled to free his bound hands to swat away the bug, a feeling of helplessness swept over him. He could feel a bite on his neck and imagined the resulting itch or irritation. "Goddamit! Where the hell am I?" He swore loudly. Anger began to replace the helplessness, and he thrashed about, kicking his bound legs to the right and left until they made contact with an object.

"Uhhh," came a soft moan.

"Shaner, that you?"

"Uhhh, damn!"

It was Shaner. Sighing with relief, Benton gently prodded the man with his boot. "Come on! Listen! Concentrate! You okay? Speak to me."

Shaner tried to sit up, using his bound hands as leverage. "My head is exploding."

"It'll get better. Try not to think about it," Benton said.

"I can't think at all," Shaner replied, paused for a few seconds and then asked, "What happened? Where are we?"

Benton wished he could answer the questions. "I think we were drugged. We're in some sort of room . . . maybe in a sustainer house like you thought."

"I feel like hell, and to top it off the floor's wet," Shaner complained.

"Is it wet, or is it just cold? It's hard; that's for sure. Seems like stone or concrete." Benton scooted closer to a wall and pressed his face against it. The wall felt damp, but he finally decided it, too, was merely cold. "I think it feels wet because there's no heat in here, probably hasn't been any heat in here for a long time."

"Well, it must be an abandoned sustainer house, then. If anyone lived here, they'd have to have heat or he'd freeze," Shaner reasoned. "Wait a minute; I thought the Bureau tried to tear down all houses that were in too bad a shape for sustainers to use part of the time."

"Thought so, Bill. However, maybe they missed some. Maybe sustainers were using this years ago and then moved into newer sustainer huts. Maybe this was just left standing, like the old woman's house. Maybe it was used by an elderly sustainer who died, and no one from the Bureau remembered it was here. Maybe no one just bothered to get rid of this place." It was quiet for a few minutes as they both tried to get their thoughts together. "But you know," Benton continued, "I don't think we're in the house – not the main part of the house. I think we're in the cellar."

"The what?"

"The basement. A basement or cellar was a lower part of a house built into the ground under the house." Benton attempted to explain the concept to Shaner. "Lots of homes had them in earlier times. Like in Babel-ON, the basement, the lower level, housed the heating and electrical systems, the sewer, workshops – whatever." Benton felt that this was not the moment to try and explain the complications of building construction to his companion.

"You mean they're up above us? We're below ground?" Shaner's voice became alarmed.

"Well, yes, I guess so. That's if they are still in the place, of course."

As if on cue, as soon as Benton finished speaking, a door opened at the end of the room, and the boy they had been chasing entered. In his hand was a lantern which lit up the drab gray walls and floor, and they could make out another figure behind him. Benton and Shaner stared in disbelief.

"Christ!" Shaner's voice exploded in the silence. "It's a kid. We've been trapped by children."

From behind the boy stepped a woman, her face thin and drawn. "Hardly children, gentlemen. We haven't been children for a long, long time." As the two men watched speechless, she motioned the boy out of the room. "Get the others, Jamie. Let's move them out of here and get a good look at what we caught."

As his eyes adjusted to the light, Benton could see the room they were lying in had been well-constructed of concrete, probably just before or during the Cycle of Chaos. That would mean it was now probably at least thirty-five years old and beginning to need some repair. It was crowded with furniture – a large table, several mismatched chairs, shelves covered with various items, and what looked like two wood stoves. Benton was intrigued by the stoves. He remembered one from his childhood in a cabin his grandparents owned – a huge black thing that his grandfather stoked with logs he cut from nearby dead cottonwood trees and which cast a warm glow through a glass inset. "Cottonwood burns hot," he could recall his grandfather saying, "but not as long as hardwoods."

"Who are you people?" Benton asked as he looked at the assembled group and struggled to sit up.

"Who we are doesn't matter," a woman responded quickly.

Obviously she must be in charge Benton thought. He recognized her voice and realized she was the one who gave directions to cut them down from the tree.

"Where are we?" Shaner began but was quickly cut off by the same woman.

"Where you are also doesn't matter. You're our prisoners and will remain so. We will not harm you if you do not try to escape."

"Escape!" Shaner exclaimed. "I can't even sit up. How can I escape?"

"Jamie, you and Michael help the two lean against that wall. Then all of you go into the other rooms. I want to talk with these two."

When the rest of the group – at least ten Benton had counted – left what he thought was a kitchen, the woman sat on the floor across from the two sustainers. *Must be in her mid-twenties* Benton thought. *Hard to guess her age though as she's so dirty. Well, unkempt at least. That hair doesn't look like it has seen a comb for months, her clothes appear to have a layer of grime on them, and she has an unpleasant odor.* He sniffed slightly and wrinkled his nose.

"Don't have the luxury of bathing," the woman said, apparently aware of Benton's distaste. "Guess you'll get use to the smell, however, as you're not going anywhere."

"They'll come looking for us," Shaner exclaimed. "Then you'll be in big trouble."

"Haven't found us for many, many years," the woman snapped. "What makes you think this time will be any different?"

"You just wait and see. You can't keep us tied up . . ." Shaner responded, but Benton interrupted. He knew they were in no position to antagonize the woman.

"Who are you and where are we?" Benton asked. He still couldn't quite believe that he and Shaner had been taken captive by people who were still living outside the towers. In spite of the situation the two men were now facing, Benton couldn't help but feel a sense of satisfaction that Solomon John had been wrong about anyone being on the outside.

"You're in our habitat which is mostly underground," the woman began, "and although it's of no importance, my name is Margot. I'm in charge."

"Underground? How was this place built? When was it built? Who built it?" Benton shot the questions at the woman.

Margot got up and settled in one of the chairs. Benton estimated that she was just over five feet tall with blue eyes and a mouth that seemed too small for her face. Like the rest she was heavily bundled up in layers of clothing.

"You don't need to know anything about this place," Margot replied. "What you do need to know is that we don't plan to harm you as long as you don't try to escape. We'll need to keep you tied up for a time until you get used to living here. Actually until the snow begins. I'm certain you two are not stupid enough to run in the snow."

No Benton thought. *She's right. We're not stupid enough to be outside during the winter months. If we can't get out of here within the next few days, we're here until next spring or summer.* He looked at Shaner who seemed to be unable to follow the woman's comments or to grasp the reality of their present situation.

"Bill! Bill!" Benton finally got Shaner to look at him. "You're okay. You're fine. We are both fine," Benton emphasized. "We are not hurt, other than a few scrapes and bruises. Do you understand what I'm saying?"

"Uh, yeh," Shaner finally responded. He looked at the woman. "You won't hurt us?"

"No," Margot replied, "if you don't try to get away. Look, here comes Jamie and Michael with the things from your stay in the house."

The two men watched as their sleeping bags and lantern were lugged in by Jamie. Michael, handsome, nearly six feet tall and with shaggy blonde hair, brought up the rear with the food supplies. "I think we got everything, especially the food," Jamie said.

At the word food, the people waiting in a nearby room burst into the kitchen area. "Oh, let's see what they have," one of the girls shouted, pushing Jamie out of the way and reaching for the supplies. "Let's see. Let's see!"

Margot restrained the girl by grabbing her around the waist and holding up her hand to fend off the others. "Stop, all of you!" she commanded. "Michael and I will sort through their packs. We cannot just immediately eat everything that we find. We need to be very careful."

There was some grumbling, but the others did as they were told, arranging themselves around a large table as Margot and Michael carefully unpacked Benton and Shaner's supplies. Almost everything was dehydrated and packaged in clear plastic containers with labels giving directions for preparation.

"You have to have hot water to prepare the food," Benton began . . .

"I know that," Margot snapped. "We still have some dry stuff."

"We even have a few cans left," Jamie interrupted, "but most were ruined."

Cans. Benton couldn't believe he had heard Jamie correctly. *Where would they get cans of food,* he wondered. Food had not been processed in cans for decades. Although most of the old canned food could still be consumed by humans, usually it had little taste or nutritional value. Sometimes the cans were damaged, and the food was unsafe to eat as many people had discovered during Chaos.

Jamie, Michael and I will tell these men what they need to know," Margot chided the boy for interrupting. "You and the others please leave. If you are too cold, get in your beds and try to sleep. We'll call you as soon as we get all of this figured out." Margot's voice had taken on a milder tone, but it was still a directive.

"You still have food in cans?" Benton began. "I thought all food was being processed and put dry into containers, unless, of course like the old woman, you could grow some fresh food. Where do you get your food . . . except what you steal from the fields of corn?"

Margot sighed and said, "Well, I guess this is as good a time as any to explain our situation to you. Actually, it has become your situation, too." Both she and Michael sat on the floor with the two bound men and Margot began to explain.

"If we hadn't had a catastrophe, you would never have found out we were here. We've been living here for many years now and doing quite well until the extremely heavy rains began a few years ago."

"Just you children?" Benton looked incredulous.

"No, No!" Michael answered. "We all had parents and even grandparents, and they took good care of us."

"Like many people, they traveled from place to place as the towers were being built. Surely you must remember those times." Margot looked at Benton who nodded in response. "Then, when they knew they would be swept into a tower, they decided to stay outside. My grandfather was a physician and was close friends with two other men – a financial advisor and an architect. The three of them had known each other for years, been in school together, I think, and were sportsmen. You know, hunting and fishing trips together. They decided to construct a haven here along the little stream and dug a place to live into the high bank."

"They built this place themselves?" Shaner finally asked. "You all lived here in this cave?"

Both Margot and Michael laughed at his question. "I know it doesn't look like much now," Michael said, "but it was very nice originally. Mr. Jacobs was a great architect and knew all about construction. The place was much larger than what you see now and continued way back into the hill. It was not as damp as it is now. We used to have heat and water just like people always did. Mr. Jacobs set up everything from solar power in the side of the bank."

"So where are your grandparents and parents now?" Benton asked.

"Dead!" Margot replied. "All dead – all of the elders — and some of the younger people, too. For years everything ran smoothly. The elders made sure there was a huge amount of food stored, and they supplemented that by hunting and fishing. The older boys went with the men, and we girls gathered berries, Morrell mushrooms, wild asparagus, a bit of the corn – whatever we could find. We kept to the woods and went out very early in the morning or after sunset so that the sustainers would not find us. Everything seemed okay until a particularly heavy rain caved in a section of the haven – the area where the elders were and four of the other rooms. Everyone was sleeping. It was the middle of the night. We couldn't get them out. We tried . . ." Margot stopped talking, a catch in her throat.

"Mud got them," Michael said, shaking his head. "Just piles of mud smothered them. All of the old ones, our other brother, Lauren's two brothers, Lucille's sister and brother . . ." He hesitated momentarily. "Some of the others . . . I've almost forgotten how many. I have to think hard to recall their names."

"As you can see," Margot continued, "this leaves us with almost no males – just Michael and Jamie, although he's only a boy. We've really had to struggle without any men to help us, to do any heavy work . . ."

Until now Benton thought. *Now you've caught yourself two males to fill in the gap left by the disastrous rain.* "You mean that you plan to keep us as prisoners to help you continue living here," he exclaimed.

"What? What?" Shaner roused himself. "I can't stay here. I need to get back to Babel-ON. You can't hold us."

"We can and we will," Margot replied. She realized that while Shaner would continue to protest their captivity, Benton fully understood that they were no longer in control of their destiny.

The late evening meal, if one could call it that, was sparse. Lauren and a little girl named Margaret, or Maggie as she was called, divided small portions from the two sustainers's rations. There was also some sort of gruel with a few berries in it.

"What is this stuff?" Shaner complained. "I've never seen anything like this in my entire life. Am I supposed to eat it?"

"It's that or go hungry," Michael replied quietly.

"Bill, it's made from corn ground into almost a powder," Benton explained to his partner. "It won't hurt you, and if you don't eat, you'll be awfully hungry by morning."

Both men were still bound at their ankles, but their hands had been freed so they could eat. "After all," Michael had said as he helped untie their feet, "there's really no place for you to go in the dark."

"It's hot food," Jamie broke into the conversation. "Margot lit a fire so we could have this, and we'll have some hot tea later."

Benton could tell this meager meal was somewhat of a treat for the young boy. "You don't often have a fire," he asked.

"No," Margot stated. "We have to be very careful that a sustainer might be in the field and see a wisp of smoke. We can have a small fire tonight as the sustainers are out of the fields earlier now that winter is almost here. Also, the smoke doesn't show up much when it's really dark. Sometimes during the summer months we can have fire if Mrs. Yates is cooking something in her house as no one would be suspicious of any smoke. She doesn't do that often though."

"Mrs. Yates." Benton stared at Margot. "You know the old woman?"

No one answered his question, but Benton immediately knew the answer and began to mull it over in his mind. *So the outsiders knew the old woman. Of course. That's why they were still able to remain in the haven. Crafty old lady. She knew they were stealing her corn – may even have encouraged them to do so. Still, she knew she would have to report some loss just to keep the Bureau happy. You could only chalk up so much loss to animals.* He laughed quietly. *Wonder if she cooked corn on the cob for them like she did for Bill and me*

As Jamie had predicted, when the evening food was consumed and the room put in some sort of order, hot tea was served to everyone. Benton noted that the cups varied in size and material. Several were made of porcelain and decorated with some floral motif; two appeared to be made of what looked like tin. Benton couldn't be certain as he hadn't seen tin cups since he was a young boy and would go camping with his grandfather. Several others were made of wood, and Benton wondered if Michael or one of the dead men had carved them from a tree branch.

As he looked around the group, he was amazed at how different the individuals looked from those that lived in a tower. First, they were all extremely thin, emaciated almost. Second, with one exception, they all had blue eyes with mops of hair varying in color from blonde to light auburn. All had skin that appeared to be a sort of gray in color. *Of course; lack of sunlight, but there's something else that makes them seem the same. What is it?* Suddenly the answer came: *Dirt! They're covered with layers of grit and dirt. They can't shower every day like we do in the towers. Wonder if they ever bathe?*

He tried also to guess their ages. It was clear that Maggie was one of the youngest of the girls but he was not certain how young. Lauren and Lucille appeared to be in their early teens. Anna was obviously the oldest, but, as with Maggie, he wasn't certain just how old. He would learn later that all of the survivors of the accident had been born in the haven but were not certain of their ages. Margot and Michael had been youngsters when the haven was being constructed but could vaguely remember that period of time. They could also recall the births of their younger siblings. Benton quickly saw that Anna, the oldest, was of little help to the rest of the group. Physically she was a member of the group, but she seemed totally apart from the others. Benton had never heard her speak nor did she do any of the required work chores. She sat close to the small fire, rubbing her hands and softly crooning to herself.

"Anna had a bad time of it," was how various members explained the woman's actions when Benton questioned them.

Margot was more forthcoming with an explanation. "When the accident happened, Anna was buried for a short time under debris including a large piece of furniture. This gave her a small amount of air, enough to keep her alive, and she frantically tried to claw her way out. We could hear her moaning and eventually were able to get to her and pull her out, but she couldn't speak, or at least she has never spoken since."

Another thing that Benton found odd was that the group leader was Margot. He wondered if Michael felt this was the way it should be or if he might resent being the oldest male and taking orders from a woman. He guessed Jamie must not care, and it appeared as if all of the others accepted Margot's wishes or commands. *Guess that's what Shaner and I will have to do also* he thought as he watched the group begin to settle for the night.

"We have to bed down early," Michael explained. "Still have a bit of oil for a lamp but as you can see, candles are what we mostly use for light, and we are running short of them."

Chapter Twelve

$\mathcal{A}$lthough it seemed to Benton and Shaner that during their confinement time stood still, they knew that many days had gone by. For one thing, they could see how dirty each had become. Since it had to be carried from the stream, water was to be used only for drinking and cooking, not bathing. In addition, neither man had shaved since their capture, and both were beginning to develop beards which tended to itch. While Shaner's retained the auburn color of the man's hair, Benton noted in a cracked mirror that his beard was showing a considerable amount of gray.

Both men were aware that the Bureau had sent out searchers to find them, or at least to find their bodies, as their captors whispered to each other of the need to be extra careful if they ventured outside the haven. The more positive part of their days was that the two had been released from their bonds and were permitted to move about the cramped living quarters and, accompanied by Michael, taken outside briefly to relieve themselves. Built into the side of the embankment was a toilet seat of sorts which drained its contents into the stream way below the "haven" as Margot referred to their abode. In this way its contents would not pollute the drinking water. Benton marveled at the construction of the toilet as well as the living quarters and wondered how the parents had been able to secure, mix and poor enough concrete to build the place. *How did they find this location: How could they obtain the materials? Why didn't someone notice what they were doing? How did they get stuff out here?* His thoughts tumbled one after another, and he wondered if he would ever have the answer to all of them. He doubted that either Michael or Margot would have been old enough to recall all of the details.

Although they had been granted more freedom, the two sustainers were never left entirely alone. *Don't know where they think we could go if we did escape* Benton thought. *It's not like we could just waltz back to the Bureau of Sustenance.* Still both men were glad to be somewhat free and to be tolerated, if not totally accepted, by their captors.

Then, one evening as the group was assembled before time for sleep, Margot suddenly announced that they would begin having a fire each night to help ward off the growing chill that permeated their quarters. "Just a very, very small fire," she had emphasized. "After all, we don't want to have to go outside any more often than necessary, and we have a meager store of wood that could quickly be depleted."

So winter's here, right?" Benton asked Margot.

"Yes, it is," she replied quietly, not meeting his eyes, "until at least late next April."

"We're alone," Shaner stated, his voice breaking. "All alone. No one's gonna find us."

"Well, you're not alone exactly," Margot indicated the others in the room, "but you are right. No one from outside will find you. We've been keeping very careful watch, and no one has been near these fields for over a week now. Mrs. Yates has returned to her sustainer sub-tower. There's already been a light snowfall, and ice is forming close to the stream bank."

The three were silent for a few minutes until Shaner finally asked. "And food? What are you — we going to do for food now?"

"Oh, we'll get by; however, I can tell you that rations are going to be pretty scanty and unappetizing. We've already eaten most of the food you two had when captured. We just will have to make do with the bits left over from before and what we were able to gather from the fields this summer."

"And next year," Benton asked, "and the year after that? What happens then? You've now got the two of us to feed, and the Bureau will send more people down here next season. Mrs. Yates won't be able to fend all of them off with her story of animals eating her corn, so you being able to gather much corn will be more difficult if not impossible."

For a few minutes Margot was silent. "You're right, of course." She sighed. "We've got to come up with a better food supply. Not just for us, but for you two additional people. We used to set some crude traps and occasionally catch small animals — rabbits, field mice . . .

"Mice!" Shaner yelped. "Mice! You eat mice?" He looked nauseaous.

"Not often," Margot replied, "as they are very hard to catch. Still, when you are hungry enough, you'll eat almost anything. If the corn we've gathered begins to mold, we'll wash off the mold and eat it. When the few berries we've stocked up get hard and dry, we'll soften them up with water. We'll eat anything we can get to eat. How do you think we've survived all this time? Do you have any idea how hard it's been to just keep us all alive?" Her voice became shrill. "Do you still think you're in a tower? Do you think you will ever again be in a tower? How do you think you are going to survive if we don't share with you what little food we have — mice, rats, snakes if we can catch them?"

Benton could see that the woman was close to becoming hysterical. "Okay, okay," he began, holding up his hands to soothe Margot. "Shaner didn't mean to get you so upset. He just doesn't understand as he has always lived in a tower, thought he'd always live there. We'll eat anything you are willing to give us and be glad for it."

Taking a deep breath, Margot calmed down although she didn't apologize for her outburst. "I'll try to think of some way to get us fed" was all she said as she left them.

Benton could see by the look on Shaner's face that he needed some kind of reassurance that their predicament was not hopeless, although he felt that might well be the case. "Remember, Bill, you asked me once if I had ever done any hunting. Well, I hunted a bit. I could still do that if I can get out of here. I could also set some traps, maybe do better than these kids, maybe catch something better than mice. Wonder if they might have kept our rifles and the shells. Maybe I could shoot something bigger."

"What?" Shaner asked. "What could you shoot that would feed all of us?"

"Well, a deer maybe. Not sure if I'd know how to skin one or preserve the meat, but it would be worth a try."

"And how you gonna do that when you are locked away down here?" Shaner asked, shaking his head as though the idea was absurd.

"Good point," Benton answered. "I'll have to talk it over with Margot. She could send the two boys to watch me. She'd know I wouldn't run off and leave you here alone. You know that, too, don't you? Besides, it's winter. I couldn't get far before I'd freeze. Also, I'm not even sure where we are now or where a sustainer tower is."

"Might work," Shaner replied after a few seconds, "but tell me how you'd make a trap, where you'd put it. Would you get enough so we wouldn't starve? What if you got hurt while outside. What would I do then? What would they do with me . . . ?"

"Whoa, whoa," Benton held his hands up to stop Shaner's rush of words. When the man became calmer, Benton quietly explained in great detail how he would trap animals, how he bet he could get a deer or a coyote or raccoon, meat which would supplement their meager supplies. Remembering what he had read as a young boy, he explained how they could cut the meat into small strips and possibly get it dried somehow so it wouldn't immediately spoil, how they could add it to the supply of corn and make a hot soup. As he talked, Shaner became less agitated.

"It'll all work out, Bill. You'll see. We're gonna be fine." Benton assured his partner, but privately he wondered if they all wouldn't starve before summer came again.

As the days dragged on and the monotonous rations became ever more sparse, Benton asked Margot where they had originally gotten food before they began to raid the corn fields.

"When the accident occurred, some of the food supplies were outside the part that caved in," Margot began.

"I'd still like to know more about the cave-in?" Benton said. "You all must have been here years before that happened. Was it just the rain?"

"Yes, it was just the rain. It had rained for several days. Maybe the dirt above just got soaked more than usual. Maybe the roof just couldn't support the extra moisture. And, yes, we had been here many years when it happened." Margot stopped speaking, and Benton could see a tear beginning to move down her cheek. Quickly she brushed it away.

"I'm sorry," Benton began. "I didn't mean to ask the wrong questions or keep going over the same subject." He could see that Margot was trying hard not to cry. "I know it must have been difficult for you . . ."

"Difficult!" Margot shook her head. "Difficult! You can't imagine it. It was awful — mud and water everywhere. It happened at night while we were all asleep, and it was so dark. We were all crying — me, too. We could hear Anna calling for help, but that was all. Other than her screams and Jamie sobbing for his mother, everything was silent. We didn't know what was happening, didn't know what to do . . . simply huddled together in the dark and waited until it began to get light."

Margot held her hands out toward Benton in a gesture of helplessness and stopped speaking. Benton remained silent. He knew there was nothing he could say that would wipe away her memories of the tragedy and wanted to give her a few minutes to regain some composure. Finally, he said.

"I'm sorry, Margot. I truly am. I can't imagine what all of you have been living with — the memory of that night."

Actually he wished to know a great deal more about the cave-in as he had the proverbial million questions. Had the survivors attempted to dig out anyone except Anna but were unable to do so? Were all of the bodies – the others – still entombed in part of the haven? No one had mentioned any kind of burial. In fact, except for this mention of Jamie crying for his mother, little had been said about their kinship other than that some had lost sisters or brothers. How were his captors all related? There had to be more than one set of parents for surely a couple couldn't have produced this many off-spring. Margot had mentioned the three adult males who had built the haven, and now he recalled that Margot had mentioned three sets of parents. Were there people other than the parents she had alluded to buried by the mudslide – adults and youngsters? He had learned that Margot, Michael and Jamie were siblings, but what of the others? Which ones in the surviving group of females were sisters?

Although he and Shaner had been permitted to move about in two of the three rooms but not the original entryway he remembered from the capture, he realized there had to be other rooms, but he did not know how many or how far back into the hillside the haven had originally been constructed. However, this was not the moment for all of his questions. He would bide his time and try to get more of the story of these outsiders later.

———

Living below ground in the confines of the haven had caused Benton to lose track of time. He reasoned that by now it must be the end of September. He looked around and saw that Shaner and Noreen were adding a bit of fuel to the fire. *Hmmm* he thought. *Looks like he's getting cozy with her. Not sure if that's a good thing. On the other hand, he has stopped talking to me all the time about a way to get out of here. Might be a good idea if he gets more involved . . .*

"Penny for your thoughts," Noreen asked.

Benton had not heard that expression for years and wondered if it had been used at one time in the haven by the elders. He remembered that his mother often used it when he seemed to be daydreaming.

"Nothing special," Benton answered, smiling at the girl. "Just wondering if we have enough wood as it's only going to get colder and colder."

"Better talk with Margot and Michael about that," she replied, a frown appearing on her forehead. "They've taken good care of us so far you know."

Benton agreed and went into the other room where Lauren and Margot were attempting to air the bedding. Close sleeping quarters provided more warmth for the sleepers, but they also had a foul odor from both the unwashed linen and bodies, an odor that even seeped into the kitchen area.

It did not appear to be the right time to discuss heating the haven, so Benton waited until two days later to again approach Margot and Michael about wood for the stove and also the extent of the group's food supply. He decided to include Jamie in the conversation as he felt that would keep Margot from becoming as upset as she had been previously when she had explained about the catastrophe.

"So how did you all feed yourselves to begin with?" Benton asked.

"There were still many cans of food and a fairly large store of dried supplies," Michael explained. "The elders had put together huge stockpiles, and we survivors ate what was not ruined. Other than a few ears of corn now and then, we hadn't gathered much from the fields until the past three years when we could see the original supplies were quickly dwindling."

"You didn't try to dig anything out of the cave-in area?" Benton asked.

"Oh, no," Margot shivered. "We couldn't bear to do that. We just couldn't bear to find what was still in there.

"It was just better to leave things as they were," Jamie interrupted hastily. "I'm not sure we could have dug our way into all of the other rooms anyway. Besides, what good would have come of it?"

Benton didn't answer immediately. *Might still be some good food in there if the cans were not damaged. Wonder if they would have begun to corrode. If not, it might be worthwhile to do some digging. Probably would have to be done by Shaner and me – maybe Michael – as I don't think Margot is up to that emotionally. She wouldn't want to have to see what remained of the ones killed in the cave-in. Probably couldn't handle that. Well I'll wait a few weeks, but then I'm going to see what I can dig out. But I won't go into that now. Not the right time.*

"You're probably right, Michael," Benton agreed with the young man. I imagine it would cause more harm than good – bring back bad memories . . . Besides I don't know how many rooms you're talking about."

"Oh, there were two other rooms as large as the kitchen and several smaller ones – like large closets – for sleeping," Michael explained. "We all shared sleeping quarters except for the elders. They each had a separate room all to themselves."

"Were the larger rooms used for something special?" Benton asked.

"Nope! Just mainly for a meeting and for school," Jamie said. "I don't miss school."

"You had a school?"

"Yes, Mr. Benton," Margot answered, emphasizing the *mister.* The parents knew it was important that we were educated – as much as was possible down here. You probably noticed that there are some books in the kitchen."

Benton had noticed the books – seven in number – and had glanced at their titles. All but one – a Bible — had seemed to be about survival. There was none of the literature that he was used to reading in Babel-ON. He could tell by her tone of voice that Margot thought he was patronizing them. "I didn't mean anything," Benton began, "I just thought it odd that you would have time for school."

"We made time," Michael emphasized, "and it helped fill time. Since we had to be in the haven most of the time, school helped fill the days. It was especially hard for the younger ones as there wasn't much room for them to play – not much physical activity permitted that would use up excess energy. We were taught to read and were told about how things had been on the outside — history I guess you could call it. We learned about practical things that would help us if we were outside, what foods in the fields and woods were edible; what first aid to give in case someone got hurt or sick. Of course, the older children all took turns helping the elders with the cooking and cleaning. It had to be that way since we could be safely out of the haven only at rare times."

"You'll get to see how well everything works," Margot added. "You'll come to accept our way of living and maybe even get to like it."

If it means I will never again have to live in Babel-ON or any other tower, I'll gladly accept this lifestyle Benton thought, but he only said, "I guess I'll have to accept it."

Although he had not thought to make some sort of crude calendar, Benton was certain that at least another month had passed, and it was now October. During the past few weeks, Benton could see that a change had gradually come over Shaner. Most of this was due, he could tell, to Noreen spending time with the man. Instead of complaining constantly, as he had done earlier, now Shaner could be heard occasionally laughing. Apparently, his partner was beginning to accept their captivity. *Not that he has much choice* Benton mused. *Still, it's better for me. Makes my life much easier here if he becomes interested in one of the girls. Means that's a worry off my mind as it seemed at first that he simply could not adjust to the drastic change from our former lifestyle in the tower.*

If Shaner's growing acceptance of their situation made life easier for Benton, the inadequate food supply constantly preyed on his mind. One day he casually approached Margot with the idea of his going outside to find food. He knew it would take some persuasion on his part.

"You know I'm right," he explained calmly as he helped her move wood nearer to the stove. "We've got to have more food, **much more food**. Maybe I can find something, trap something ... In addition, we need to get more water to bathe or at least to wash our hands and faces or we're all going to be ill. You people haven't been this dirty always, have you?"

"No," Margot replied, glancing at her hands and fingernails which were encrusted with soil. "Until this year we'd been able to tap into the tanks originally used for water storage, but they ran dry. In the accident, the lines to the creek were broken, and no more water came into the tanks. Also, we haven't any power now to run the pumps even if the water lines were intact. I guess I just didn't see how dirty we all were."

Or didn't want to see Benton thought. However, it wasn't his intention to humiliate her or to alienate her. The group badly needed both water and food. "Well, we're all dirty now," Benton gave a small laugh, "but maybe Michael and I can somehow make that better."

"I'll have to talk your proposal over with the rest of the group," Margot began. "They may not feel it safe to allow you that much freedom."

Benton knew this was just Margot stalling for time. As far as he could tell, she made all of the major decisions and had probably done so since the accident. *Funny* he thought, *she always calls the cave-in of the haven an accident. So do the others. Wonder why. Could they have prevented it? No, I doubt there was much they could do. It was simply an accident of nature.*

"Fine," he said abruptly as he could see Margot was waiting for a reply. "You let me know what's decided."

It was only one day before Margot approached Benton and Shaner about one of them leaving the haven to search for food. "One of you can go," Margot said as she and Michael sat with the two men. "But, Michael has to go with you, and he's agreed to do so. I assume Shaner is agreeable to staying in the haven."

"What choice do I have?" Shaner asked. "If I don't agree, Benton can't go, and we'll all be worse off. Besides I have no idea how to hunt or trap anything."

"Well, there's no guarantee that I can either," Benton said hastily. "I want that understood now. I haven't hunted in a very long time. I'll do the best I can, but . . ." He left the sentence dangling.

Michael broke in. "Our biggest problem is not your hunting or trapping skill. Our biggest problem will be not freezing to death. I went out yesterday just for a brief minute. There's several feet of snow everywhere with temperature mostly below zero. Didn't see any living thing near the haven."

"Any tracks?" Benton asked. "Anything at all?"

"Well, I did see where something, some animal, tried to brush a spot in the snow down by the stream."

"Good," Benton replied, nodding at Michael. "That's what I need to know. Four eyes are always better than two," he added, hoping Michael would consider his words a pat on the back.

"And water," Margot broke in. "What about more water?"

"Michael and I will each get a pail full of snow – ice if we can break it off of something – as soon as we are out of the haven," Benton replied. "We'll come right back inside to warm up a bit, then go out again and get more snow in another bucket. Then we'll do that again, several times. You'll need immediately to thaw out what we bring in, as the melted snow will make less than a bucket. This means getting a lot of buckets full of snow. However, if we do this repeatedly for just one morning, we should have enough water to clean all of us up a bit. We'll try to carry in a fair amount of water at least once a week."

"Food," Shaner interrupted. "I can stay dirty and my stomach doesn't care about that. What about more food?"

"We won't spend the entire time getting snow for water," Benton replied. "I'll set some of the traps you and I put together. Try to catch a squirrel or rabbit." Benton made certain he didn't mention mice. "If Michael and I go out every day for a week, we might see something big to shoot – a hawk, maybe a deer. I'd even shoot a squirrel or rabbit if I see one, although I hate to use our bullets on small game."

"Would there still be some corn cobs under the snow — a few that were not harvested and have dried up?" Margot asked.

"Might be, but we'd have to dig for them. Also, the animals would have been digging for any food they could find. We could try; however, I think it would be a waste of our time."

"What about tracks?" Michael asked. "Won't we have to be careful that we don't leave tracks for someone to find?"

"Who?" Benton looked at the young man. "Who do you mean? There isn't a soul out there now. Margot knows that or she wouldn't let me out of here."

"That's true," Margot said, placing her hand on Michael's arm and smiling at him. "It's not like it is during the summer months when the sustainers are nearby. There's no one out there to see you – no one out there to call for help if you get into any kind of trouble or become injured. Now it will be just you and Benton," she paused, "and a big, lonely world of frigid white."

Chapter Thirteen

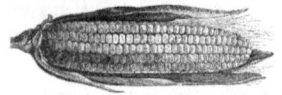

*C*old? Benton could not recall ever having been so cold. Even with the heavy clothing he and Shaner had brought with them from the tower plus extra clothing from the haven underneath his coat and pants, Benton knew that he could only stay outside brief periods of time. Two pairs of gloves helped some, but extra socks did not keep his feet from feeling numb. He knew that Michael was also suffering from the intense cold although the boy never complained. It was mid-November, at least five months before the cold weather would relinquish its hold on the country. *A tower would sure look good to me now* Benton thought and then laughed. He had wanted to be outside the towers, had worked it so Solomon John would send Shaner and him back to the fields. *In the summer, in the summer when it's hot and everything is green and alive. Not like this, white and frozen. No color now . . . just the white snow and the gray, lifeless trees. Well, I asked for it, and now I've got it . . .*

"What's so funny?" Michael asked as he struggled to keep up with Benton. "I don't see anything to laugh about out here.

If we don't get back inside soon, we'll be frozen like that ice on the creek."

Benton knew Michael was right. They had been outside for over two hours, and it was becoming ever more difficult to breathe in the cold air. So far, the traps Benton had set in the thicket over the past few days had yielded up only four rabbits. Scrawny ones at that but better than nothing. The previous week they had trapped two squirrels and today were lucky to find a frozen one lying beside a tree. *Haven't even seen a deer* Benton thought. *Or a coyote. Wonder if coyotes taste good. Or a bobcat . . . maybe they taste good. Well, what does it matter how they would taste. We haven't caught one yet.*

"I'm freezing," Michael exclaimed suddenly. "I mean it; I think I'm freezing. I can't feel my hands."

"Okay. Let's go back. We have a bit of meat to show for our efforts today if we can thaw it out. Let's grab a pail of snow each so there will be extra water to cook this thing in."

The two men began to retrace their steps when there was a loud crack. Benton immediately dropped to the ground and yelled at Michael who was looking around in astonishment.

"Get down!" Benton screamed. "Dammit, get down!"

As the young man dropped in the snow, Benton cautiously peered into the surrounding woods. Nothing moved. There was no other sound. As far as he could tell, the two men were alone.

"What was that? What was that?" Michael asked, his voice quavering.

"Thought it was a shot," Benton replied. *A shot? How could it be a shot? There was no one in the woods except Michael and himself.*

"Nothing, I guess," Benton said as he got to his feet and helped Michael to stand. "Thought it sounded like someone shooting, but that's ridiculous. We're the only ones out here. Probably just a noise from a branch loaded with snow and ice breaking off a tree. Nothing for us to worry about." However, the sound as loud as a gunshot had unnerved Benton, and he urged the young man to hurry toward the sanctuary of the haven.

"We'll come out again tomorrow," Benton said. "Maybe have better luck than we've had these past few weeks."

As they gathered some snow in the buckets sitting outside the haven, Benton casually surveyed the area around them. He didn't wish to worry Michael, and he cautioned the young man not to mention their scare to Margot.

The others welcomed the two men back inside, and the squirrel was immediately placed in a large pot to thaw. "With some corn added, we'll have a good stew," Margot said.

"But it won't taste very good," Jamie complained. "There isn't any taste to anything we eat any more. Everything tastes the same."

"Well, tell you what," Margot began. "Let me check what's left in our pantry. I think there still are a few cans of tomatoes on the shelves. I know they are several years old, but I don't think they will poison us if we eat them. We'll just add one can to the squirrel stew to give it a little flavor."

"Wish we had some carrots and onions. Mrs. Yates always added that to her stew," Lauren put in.

So Mrs. Yates cooked for them Benton mused. *First time I've heard this. Wonder how long that went on. She must have been aware that the haven was here for years before most of the adults were dead. Had she socialized with them . . . cooked for them also? Of course, she cooked for Shaner and me. Why wouldn't she cook for them . . .*

Benton's thoughts were interrupted as Margot returned with a tin can, its label torn and peeling. However, a small portion of the label clearly showed the picture of a tomato. He watched Margot laboriously open the can and add its contents to the already simmering meal. He realized that the group had been fortunate to survive as long as they had with only the stolen corn, the little food that survived the accident and what Mrs.Yates' had been able to do to help. Nevertheless, their survival time in the haven was rapidly running out.

Chapter Fourteen

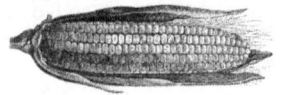

*Y*ou're going to have to leave here," Benton said to Margot in December, a day that he had been outside and lucky enough to recover several small animals from his traps. "I know I got that one deer, but we consumed every bit of it within two weeks. So far I haven't even seen another. I'll try to find and shoot others, but getting any kind of meat is iffy at best. You need to think soon about leaving the haven."

"I have thought about it," Margot replied, "but I'm just as confused as ever. When to go? How to go? Where to go? How to get the others to see the need to leave?"

"And" . . . Benton paused, thinking about the best way to phrase his question, "what do you intend to do about Anna? You simply can't continue to feed someone who cannot shoulder some of the responsibility for your survival. Also, you can't take someone along who can't pull her own weight on the journey. Have you thought about what you will do?"

"I don't know. How can I know now?" Margot said abruptly. "It's too soon to think about this."

"**It is not too soon**," Benton emphasized his words. "The time is growing short, and you will all have to accept that fact."

Margot was silent for a few seconds before continuing in a voice that was less curt, "Of course you're right. I know that. We can't take her with us. Actually she's not with us in the true sense; she's off in some world of her own. She'd be too great a burden on the rest of us as we'd have to watch her constantly for fear she'd wander off. She might even be found by a sustainer, and they'd know we were living outside."

"When was the last time Anna was outside the haven?" Benton asked.

"She hasn't been out of the haven since the accident. Not once. I know that sounds harsh, but it was the best thing. We couldn't watch her all the time."

"I can see that," Benton nodded in agreement, "but you will have to face making a decision soon. You can't just leave her here to starve to death, and you can't take her with you. You'll have to get rid of her."

"Get rid of her? You mean kill her? Murder her?" Margot exclaimed loudly as she stared wide-eyed at Benton.

"Shhh! Lower your voice or the others may hear you." Benton held up his hand to quiet the woman. "Think! Calm down and think! You're the leader. You have to face this problem. What is your other option?"

"I couldn't do that," Margot moaned. "I just couldn't do that to Anna. She's one of us. You don't understand. We can't get rid of her. That's an inhuman suggestion."

"It's not a suggestion," Benton stated. "It's a fact. If you wish your group to survive, you've got to make some hard decisions — very hard decisions. This is just one of them. First,

you've got to decide when to leave the haven. You've got to
decide how to travel. You can't travel in the day; you'd be seen
by a sustainer some time along the way. Then you've got to
figure out how to collect, package and tote enough food to
survive. Everyone will have to carry as much food as he or she
possibly can. If someone can't do that, he or she will be left
behind. "

Margot merely stared at him for a long time and then
asked, "Couldn't we steal enough corn to feed us as we've
always done?"

She sounds like a small child . . . like she's asking for a treat
Benton thought, but he decided it was best to try and reassure
her. "Sure, that's probably the only way you can survive, but
you'll need to leave early in May, and there'll be no corn then.
It will just have been planted and won't be ripe until late July
or early August. Possibly you can find, mushrooms, wild
onions, maybe some early berries. You won't have Mrs. Yates to
help you out as her garden won't be ready to harvest until
August, just like the corn."

Margot was silent for a long time but finally broke the
silence. "You make it sound impossible," she finally said, "and
if it were possible, I don't even know where to go. I just know
we have to leave here or we'll all die."

"Best bet would be to head south," Benton said, "where
the climate is a little milder. But if anyone's looking for you,
that's what they'd expect. Maybe head southwest . . . " He
mulled that suggestion over for a minute and then continued.
"Maybe into California where you'd be by the ocean, could
catch some fish, be able to get fruit or nuts out of the fields
without being seen. But . . ." he paused for a minute, "there's a
problem with that idea. You'd have the desert to cross with

very little chance of water or food. Best to try and settle close to water at least ..."

"So, what you're telling me is that the idea is impossible," Margot began ...

"Not impossible," Benton interrupted, "but very difficult. Extremely difficult, I'd say. Will take a lot of planning. You'd have to travel at least several miles each night, mostly in the dark. Everyone would have to pull their weight just for any of you to make it. And I mean actual weight – heavy backpacks. Some might fall behind, not make it. You'd have to face that, have to walk off and leave them behind. One thing I can tell you for sure. None of you would make it if Anna has to be dragged along."

For a moment Benton thought the woman was going to break down. She turned away from him for several minutes, working to get control of her feelings. Finally, she looked at him and said, "You're so cruel. So hard. So matter of fact about this. Anna doesn't mean anything to you. You don't even see her as a person."

She paused for a minute, and Benton didn't respond. *She's correct. As far as I'm concerned Anna is merely a liability. Without her we may have a chance. With her along, we probably can't survive.* He nearly laughed aloud. *Imagine that. I said* **we**. *I guess I'm beginning to think I belong to the clan.*

"Unfortunately, I know you're right," Margot began, interrupting his reverie, "although I hate to admit it. I'll talk with Michael about this, and it'll be our decision – just Michael's and mine. Not yours, do you understand? We'll do what's necessary, but the others must not know anything about this discussion. When the time comes, we'll tell them. That will be soon enough."

BETTY L. ALT

"I'll do what I can to help you," Benton responded in a placating manner "Let me give the problem some more thought, and see if there is any other option. We'll talk later, Margot. We still have some time. What's important now is that we have to survive **this winter** down here before you will have to solve the problem of moving out."

———————

Over the next few days Benton did give the problem of the need for additional food a great deal of thought and decided to talk with Shaner who now seemed fully reconciled to his life in the haven. Late one night as they were bedded down in the kitchen area, he broached the subject of the inadequate food supply.

"Bill, I've been thinking for quite some time now, and I want to see what you think of my idea to get us more food."

"Sure." Shaner sat up. "Do you want to see if they'll let me go outside with you to try and find something?"

"No, I want you to help me dig farther back into the haven. Margot as much as indicated that she knew there was probably additional food that might have survived the cave-in. Now it might all be ruined, but there's a fair chance that it might not be. If it is tin cans like the few that still remain here, we could dig them out. The cans the group has been using are several years old, but that doesn't seem to make them unusable."

"I'd never seen cans of food until now," Shaner said. "How long can food be edible if it's in cans?"

"Beats me, Bill, but we know if there are some buried in those other rooms, they should be as good as what we've been eating. Hasn't made us ill, has it?"

"Nope," Shaner replied, "and I'm all for seeing what we can dig out."

"Okay, tomorrow I'll tell Michael our plans to start digging. He can break the news to Margot and the others as I know it will make them uncomfortable to say the least."

It had sounded like a great idea when Benton first suggested that he and Shaner begin digging into the old part of the haven. However, very quickly they discovered that it was plugged with heavy clay-like mud and debris. Benton had hoped to be able to dig only in one area but was told by Michael that the area the elders used for storage was across from one of the larger rooms. This meant excavating the larger area first and then hoping their efforts would be rewarded by cans of food when they reached the pantry area. Also, what they dug out had to be removed from the dig and the current living quarters. Therefore, several times a day Michael and Jamie had to cart heavy buckets of dirt outside. The additional problem was that while Benton was participating in the excavation, he was not outside hunting or setting traps to add to the dwindling supply of food.

"Oh, oh!" Benton exclaimed.

"What?" Shaner yelped and moved closer to his partner.

"I think I just uncovered the sole of a shoe. Maybe we'd best dig a little further over to the right as I'm certain we've found a body."

"Oh, no," Shaner whispered. "I wonder who it is."

"Don't know and don't want to know," Benton said as he crawled to his right and began digging away from the shoe. "That's exactly why Margot said they hadn't dug in here before. They don't want to find their parents and brothers and sisters."

"Yeh," Shaner responded. "I can't imagine how hard it must be knowing they're all buried just a few feet away from where you have to live."

Benton didn't reply but he thought to himself *Shaner seems to have matured a great deal since we were first captured. He's taken on as much responsibility as they will let him have and seems less unhappy, much more content.*

"Well, let's not mention our discovery to the others," Benton said. "What they don't know won't hurt them. I've hit something else over here – a box – no, it's some kind of satchel or briefcase. Let's dig it out and see what's in it."

It took several minutes to unearth the case which turned out to be rather large and with the hinges broken. After they had cleaned it up some, Benton pried it open and discovered medical supplies which he assumed had been for treatment of various illnesses among the haven members.

"Not sure what some of these pills are for," he said to Shaner. "Wonder if either Margot or Michael would know."

"Well they must not have needed them for the past years," Shaner replied as he rummaged around in the case. "Look, what's that thing?."

"An old thermometer. It was used to see if someone had a fever. Apparently no one has had a fever," Benton nodded thoughtfully, "or if they did, I wonder if anyone was aware of it."

They continued digging, avoiding as best they could any evidence of bodies. Eventually, they came to what had been a door to a small room. When they cleared the dirt and debris they found the elders' storage place for food. While many of the cans and jars had been broken, there remained a fair number still intact.

"Is it all good?" Shaner asked immediately.

"Don't know. The cans of food seem to be fine, at least as good as the ones we've been eating from since we've been here. The falling dirt must have acted like a shield. Most are not too badly dented. If they've been split, however, we shouldn't use their contents."

"What about the other stuff – the stuff in glass?" Shaner picked up one of the jars and wiped the dirt from its sides.

"I'm not too sure about that," Benton began as he, too, wiped dirt from a jar. "I think this is some kind of pickled stuff, but see how cloudy it looks. I remember my grandmother used to can stuff every fall . . ."

"Can?" Shaner interrupted.

"Yeah. She'd cook stuff from her garden or what she bought at the store. Green beans, peaches, things like that. She'd seal the cooked food in glass jars and store it for later. Of course, she bought most of the food from the grocery store." *Wonder if any of this is making any sense to Bill* he thought. *Doubt if he can visualize a grocery store from the old days.*

"But can we eat it?" Shaner burst into Benton's thoughts. "I'm always hungry, and I know the others are, too. Can we eat it?"

"Probably not the food in the glass jars. See, the seals around the lids are not tight as they should be, and the food inside may have spoiled." He could see that Shaner didn't understand the word *spoiled.* "The food may taste bad or may have something in it that would make us all sick," he explained.

Benton separated the jars from the cans which he moved to one side of the space. Within a few minutes they had found, a large tin of oil, some salt and several large plastic barrels that contained flour.

"What can you do with flour?" Shaner asked.

"Well, you could make bread if you had the other necessary ingredients. Of course, I don't know if we do. You'd need eggs, I think, and yeast and ... well, actually I don't know what all you'd need." Benton looked at Shaner. "Doesn't seem to be any weevils in the flour. The containers must have been air tight."

"Weevils? What's a weevil?"

"Well, Bill, it's sort of a tiny bug, very tiny that sometimes gets in flour. We could pick them out if there were any or, I guess, we could just eat them. I don't think they'd hurt us."

"Ugh!" Shaner exclaimed. "I won't eat weevils, and I sure as hell won't eat mice!"

Benton was about to reply that Shaner would eat almost anything if he got hungry enough and knew that Shaner did not always know what Margot had added to their soups and stews. About that time Michael arrived to tote dirt to the outside and indicated before he left that once again snow was falling. "Coming down pretty hard. Bet we get at least another ten to twelve inches."

Benton acknowledged his comment but said, "Instead of the dirt, start taking some of this food back. Tell Margot to wait until we get done here before anyone eats anything though. We don't want anyone becoming ill."

The digging continued when suddenly Benton exclaimed, "Look, Bill. Jelly!"

"What?"

"Jelly. Apple jelly, I think, and it looks like it's still good." Benton held up a small glass jar containing a yellowish jell. "We haven't had anything that tasted sweet since we've been down here. The group doesn't have any sugar, hardly any salt."

"Yeh," Shaner replied. "What little food we get is pretty tasteless, but complaining about it doesn't do any good."

"Well, then, this should be a real treat. Let's see if we can find any more. There must be more somewhere in here."

As they dug farther, they uncovered almost a dozen small jars of jelly – one which was much darker than the others. Benton wondered if it might be grape jelly but wasn't certain that grapes grew in the area. Possibly, it could be from some other berries – strawberries or maybe even blueberries.

"What's that funny stuff on the top of the jars?" Shaner asked. "They don't have lids like the others."

"Wax," Benton replied. "Paraffin. You melted it and poured it on the top of the jelly. It sealed the air out and preserved the contents from spoilage. That's why this will be okay to eat." With a big smile, he looked over at Shaner. "Do you realize what this means, Bill? Not only have we found some food to help us through the winter months, but now we've got wax."

"So?" Shaner queried.

"You know how early we all have to go to bed," Benton began, "well that's because we can't afford to use up the little bit of oil we have left for the lamps. Also, the supply of candles is rapidly running out. I think the group has been extremely lucky to have been able to keep any light at night. Most of the light we have now is because it's winter, and Margot keeps a fire in the stove. We get a little light from that small window in front of the oven. Now we can use the wax off of the jelly glasses to add to our supply of candles until we leave the haven for good."

"Leave the haven?" Shaner's eyes grew wide and his voice became harsh. "What do you mean leave the haven? How can we leave the haven!"

Benton didn't respond to the questions, merely nodded his head and continued to dig.

Chapter Fifteen

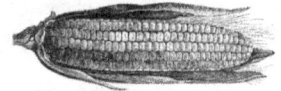

*F*inding the additional food boosted everyone's spirits, although it was still carefully rationed. Margot could hardly remember when there had been bread in the haven – certainly not since the accident. However, she managed to combine the recovered oil and flour into dough and made a form of unleavened bread. The jelly, particularly, was a big hit as the youngest members in the group had never seen nor tasted any. Having something sweet to put on a piece of bread was a real treat for them.

"Didn't find any sugar?" Noreen asked.

"Nope," Shaner replied. Could be some farther back in the cave-in, but I don't know if we are going to do much more digging. The jelly is sweet though."

Benton thought it interesting that Shaner responded so quickly to Noreen. He had noted that the two spent a great deal of the time glancing toward each other and that Noreen was the person Shaner spoke with the most. He also thought it interesting that Shaner had not mentioned his tower girlfriend Lana Howard since they had been in the haven. He would have liked to tease his partner about the growing attachment to Noreen but decided against it.

It was important that Shaner go with the group when it left the haven, Benton knew. If Shaner were definitely interested in Noreen, he felt it to be a positive result of their captivity, although he no longer felt like a captive. A few evenings earlier he had again discussed with Shaner the necessity to find another place for the group to live.

"What do you intend to do, Bill, as we are going to have to abandon this place? You could find your way back to the old woman's house and on to the road. Sustainers would find you, and you could go back to Babel-ON, back to your normal life. However, you'd need to give me your word that you'd give us time to get away and then . . .

"I'm not going back," Shaner interrupted. "I'll go with you . . . with the group. You're going to need me, need my help."

"It's not going to get any easier, Bill. We'll be on the run, have to hide, always be hungry, maybe never find a safe place."

"Yeh, yeh, I know, but you've got to admit, I've finally adapted to this life – bad as it is. I won't lie. I miss the tower and its easy way of living, but I've grown fond of this weird group. I'll stay with them, see what happens." Shaner shrugged as if he had said it all.

Benton was wise enough not to mention Noreen. He merely smiled and said, "Good! We will need an extra man."

Benton had talked with Margot and Michael, and it was decided that digging farther back into the haven would not be beneficial for anyone. The finding of the one shoe had been

mentioned only to Michael who said he did not wish to know
its owner. He also felt that it would not help the others if a
body were uncovered, explaining, "We've got enough problems just trying to survive without having to grieve over long
dead family members."

Monotonous days turned into monotonous weeks with
the adults trying to make certain of their continued survival.
Benton and Michael went out each day, hopeful that their
hunting and trapping efforts would be rewarded. Jamie and
Shaner had been given the task of gathering snow and ice for
water and adding to the fuel supply. The adult females tended
to the meals and the very necessary cleaning of their cramped
quarters. Even though they now had more heat, the haven
always felt cold and damp. To ward off this effect, the inhabi-
tants wore layers of clothing which always appeared grimy. At
least every three weeks when the odor of stale bodies became
almost overbearing, Margot insisted that some of the clothing
be washed. Of course, this meant more water would be
needed, necessitated more trips outside for Jamie and Shaner,
and filled the cramped quarters with wet clothing hanging to
dry on every piece of the scanty furniture.

Although the paraffin from the jelly glasses had added to
the supply of candles, bedtime still had to come early. To help
break the tedious routine, Benton and Shaner gathered the
youngsters around the glow from the stove and told them stories of the outside world. Before long, this also became a routine for the older members of the group as they, too, were very
interested in hearing about tower living. It was a difficult task
for the two sustainers because having lived in Babel-ON for so
long, almost all of the terms Benton and Shaner used had no
meaning for the others.

"What's a swimming pool?" Beth asked as Shaner mentioned that he and Benton usually swam each evening after their shift at the Bureau of Sustenance was completed.

"Well, it's a big pool," he replied, "a big basin that holds lots of water. It's really deep in spots. People swim in it for exercise and for fun, I guess."

"Lots of water?" Lucille looked puzzled. "Where can you get that much water?" Lucille's concept of water was the amount that the men toted in from outside – a very small amount.

Elevators, escalators, the second sun – all of these concepts were unimaginable to those in the haven. Margot, Michael and Jamie were familiar with automobiles as they had seen the sustainer trucks carting grain from the fields. However, they had no concept of how the vehicles operated.

When explaining how towerites lived became too difficult, Benton would tell about his early years outside Babel-ON. This was of particular interest to Margot and Michael as they knew the group would eventually have to be existing away from the safety of their habitat. In addition, both Benton and Shaner would relate some of the material they had learned in school – particularly literature and history.

One evening in late January as the two men prepared for the night, Benton said to Shaner, "I know it gets tiring telling and retelling all our stories, Bill, but it helps pass the time – both for us and for them. Everything we do is so routine, so mechanical and boring. Day after endless day. Nothing different ever happens down here."

Benton would remember those words a few days later when he was awakened by Michael.

"Get up! Get up! Something's wrong with Robin. Margot's with her, but we don't know what to do." Michael was kneeling by Benton;s side with a lit candle and poking him in the ribs.

Shaking his head to arouse himself, Benton asked. "What's wrong with her?"

"We don't know. She's bleeding. You've got to help her."

"Calm down," Benton said as he crawled out of his sleeping bag, one of the last remnants from his tower days. "I'll be right with you."

By that time Shaner was also awake and struggling to get up. "What? What?" he said.

"Margot and Robin need me. Apparently Robin's ill," Benton replied, noting that most of the rest of the clan had moved into the kitchen area where he and Shaner slept. Huddled near the stove in the dim light, they looked almost like apparitions. Their eyes were wide with fright, and Lauren was sobbing quietly.

When he entered the small room where Margot was attempting to help Robin, he could see the blood – more blood than he had ever seen before. He did recall seeing quite a bit of blood once when a sustainer had been injured in the fields but not to the extent that he now saw. He knew that there was nothing any of them could do to help Robin. She was dying. *A miscarriage* Benton thought, although he couldn't remember the last time he had heard that term. He was aware that it meant Robin was not going to have her baby. The main problem was that he nor the others had any medical knowledge that would help the woman. In fact, he had no idea what might have caused the miscarriage, but he immediately knew that Robin was beyond their help. Still, he had to attempt to do something.

"We've got to try and stop the bleeding," he said quietly as he didn't wish those in the kitchen to hear him. "Otherwise she's going to bleed to death."

"What's wrong with her?" Michael asked.

"Something's wrong about the baby," Benton answered, "but I'm not a doctor. I don't know what to do except try and stop her bleeding. Get me some cloths . . . now. **Now**!" He emphasized the word, and Michael hurried out of the room. Benton looked over at Margot who was cradling Robin's head in her arms and crooning softly to the woman.

"She'll be all right, won't she?" Margot asked, a catch in her voice.

Benton didn't respond, merely took the cloth from Michael when he returned and tried to staunch the flow of blood. *No, she won't be all right. She's dying, and there's nothing any of us can do to stop that. Look at her, she's no longer aware that any of us are here.* He didn't voice his thoughts, however, as he needed both Margot and Michael to remain as calm as possible.

The three of them stayed by Robin's side until it became obvious that she was dead. Finally Margot laid Robin's head down, and she and Michael just sat quietly by the dead woman. Benton could see that they were unable to accept the inevitable, especially Michael as he and Robin had been an acknowledged pair and spent as much time as was possible together. The young man kept rubbing the dead woman's hand, as if he could somehow revive her, and in a low husky voice repeatedly called her name.

"Margot," Benton murmured quietly but there was no response. "Margot," he said more sharply to get her attention. "You need to think about what's to be done."

"What?" She finally turned and looked at him, but Benton wasn't certain that she saw him. "What's to be done?"

"Why don't I stay here and you take Michael into the kitchen area," he urged. "You'll need to tell the others what has happened and try and comfort them. They're frightened now, don't know what's going on. You need to help them as I assume no one else has died before this. They won't understand . . . about death and dying."

At his urging, Margot finally helped Michael up, and the two slowly moved into the other room away from the dead Robin. Benton wasn't certain what he should do but finally drew a cover over the woman as he began to plan in his mind the necessary steps that would need to be taken. *We'll have to move her out of the haven immediately and try to clean up this room as best we can. We can take her outside, but what then? We can't dig a grave as everything is frozen or deep in snow. We can't just leave her lying in the snow; something might eat on her.* He remembered reading about, or maybe seeing in a film, how Indians buried their dead high up on poles so that animals couldn't get to the bodies. *Maybe we could do that although it would take Shaner and me a lot of time to build a place and lift the body. Cremation? Wouldn't it take a great deal of wood to actually burn all of Robin's body?*

Margot had returned to the room, followed closely by Shaner. The three of them bundled up the blood-soaked bedding on which Robin had been lying, and Shaner volunteered to be the one to move it outside. "I'll take it as far as I can and just toss it, I guess."

"Fine, tomorrow," Benton replied, "but our main problem is what to do with Robin."

"Oh, Robin," Margot crooned as she knelt beside the body. "Poor Robin. Poor, poor Robin." After a few minutes, she turned to Benton and said in a composed voice, "I'll keep the others occupied, and you and Shaner will need to carry her out. I hate it, but you must carry her as far away as you can and try to place her so that Michael won't stumble across her when he's outside."

Benton was impressed with her composure as she gave them their orders. Without speaking, he and Shaner did as they were instructed, but it was difficult work, particularly as they tried to keep the others from seeing the body. They lugged Robin's remains beyond the toilet area and unceremoniously tossed her into a narrow ravine. Benton knew that the body would be frozen within an hour and quickly covered with the unending snow.

Since the younger members had no recollection of any death, Margot did her best answering their questions. "Where has Robin gone? When will she be back?" Connie asked over and over. Although Margot patiently attempted to provide answers to the young girl, she felt certain that her explanation was inadequate.

For several days, the older members of the tribe mourned Robin's demise, especially Michael who had become unnaturally quiet. He and Benton still journeyed outside each day to hunt and check the traps, but Michael seldom commented on anything. A simple *yes* or *no* was his usual reply to Benton's questions. Sometime merely a grunt seemed to suffice, and the sustainer did not press the young man for additional conversation.

Benton could tell that Robin's death had suddenly made all of her kinsmen aware how vulnerable they were. On the other hand, Benton took a more practical approach to the woman's demise. He had realized early on that Robin's pregnancy would be a hindrance when the group had to move. No one knew for certain when she had become pregnant, and there was the possibility that she would have the infant before early spring. If that were the case, the problem was doubled – actually tripled or quadrupled. Did anyone know how to deliver a baby? Benton didn't. He assumed Robin would nurse the child, but if not, how would they provide food for it? Babies cried, he knew. Would they be able to keep it quiet enough so that a sustainer would not hear it when they were in hiding during the day? Would Robin be healthy enough to travel when it was time to leave the haven? If she didn't have the baby before they had to move, would she be strong enough to keep pace with the others? Could they cope with the birth of an infant while away from the haven? No, Benton would not mourn for Robin. In the end, her death was a blessing for the group.

Chapter Sixteen

"**T**ime to begin to get organized for the move," Benton announced to Margot early one morning in March. "By the end of April, the snow will be pretty much gone, and the days will be warmer. Nights will still be cold until late May, of course, so you'll need to wear warm clothing – several layers I imagine. Course you'll still have to carry what you take off. Clothing in itself will become a burden, but you can't just toss it aside."

"Do you think we can take bedding – blankets and such?"

"No, Margot, definitely not! That will be too heavy. During the day you can hunker down to sleep out of sight of sustainers, and you'll have to sleep in your clothes to keep warm. Then when it's warmer, you will have to shed clothing as it will be too hot. However, listen to me. You can't abandon it; you'll have to carry the clothes with you for the next winter."

Benton wondered if the group would be able to do as he suggested. Would they be able to wear the same clothing for weeks, possibly months? At least for the first month, it would be too cold to wash the clothing or bathe. Because of the temperature problem, any washing of garments, or bathing for that matter, would have to be done in the day when they might be discovered. Nights would be needed for the continued trek south, and they couldn't spare the time to stop for cleanliness. They had all been filthy when he had first seen them, so he guessed that they could survive being dirty again.

"Well, if we have to, we have to!" Margot emphasized. "You and Shaner will need to explain all of this to the others."

"We will, with your help," Benton continued. "It's probably best if you head toward south Texas, along the gulf. Your main worry is food. How you can carry enough food to keep you all alive. If you didn't set out until late July, there would be some things ready for harvest – fruit, vegetables, grains, all of the food the sustainers would begin harvesting for the towers. Still, you wouldn't have any proteins. I guess you could try to steal some eggs, but that would just be a lucky break if you could. Almost all egg production comes from chickens that are kept in huge sheds during their entire life, fed a special type of meal. I guess you might find an old sustainer like Mrs. Yates who just might have a chicken coop . . ." Benton stopped talking for a minute and then continued, "No. Wouldn't count on it, and you might be seen, get caught."

"Well, couldn't you, Bill and Michael hunt and trap," Margot asked, her voice soft and pleading. "That's what you've been doing for us all these past months?"

"Doubt it. It just would be luck if we got something. You know the old saying, 'Hunting takes a little skill and a lot of luck.'" Benton chuckled.

"No, I didn't know that." Apparently Margot did not see anything to laugh about.

"I'm sorry, Margot," Benton began as he could see that for her this was not a humorous moment. "We might be able to hunt or trap something, but usually that's done at night. Most wild animals aren't out until night, and that's when you have to travel. When you run out of the food you've taken from the haven, you're gonna have to steal, and you're gonna have to be good at it or you'll starve!"

"It sounds like you think the move is impossible."

"No," Benton was quick to emphasize his disagreement. "It's possible if it's planned well. Think. Until we leave, we should eat only food that Michael and I are able to trap or hunt and what's in cans. Cans will be too heavy to carry, so we need to keep all of the dry food for the trek. Use what's left of the flour and make bread, but keep it for the trip. That's light to carry and filling, but remember, it's for the trip. We can't eat it now. Grind up as much corn as possible and try to package it, but on the trip it will have to be eaten raw or mixed with water into a gruel. It will be too risky to have a fire, so you'll have to eat it cold. Won't be much nourishment in either the bread or corn, so I imagine you'll all lose quite a bit of weight. Just hope that no one becomes seriously ill or possibly breaks a leg or you might have to leave them. That would be bad for the group if he or she didn't die since we couldn't carry anyone. Also, if we had to leave someone behind, you know a sustainer would probably find that individual. He or she would be interrogated by the Bureau people and probably tell about the rest of us. Then there would be a massive hunt, and I doubt if we could stay hidden and elude our followers."

Even though Margot had been listening to him, Benton realized that she was simply overwhelmed by what he was saying. The group had been protected in the haven for so long that she was unable to comprehend that they would actually be leaving or to realize the difficulties which lay ahead when they had to move out. Food had been their problem; the possibility of capture had been remote.

"You and Bill will be with us, won't you?" Margot asked plaintively. "You two can show us what to do, help us stay out of trouble, not get lost . . . "

"Of course, of course," Benton replied quickly. "I'm just giving you some of the worst possibilities. It will all work out well. You'll see."

His words seemed to ease Margot's anxiety a bit, but he could tell that she was still resistant to what he had outlined for the move. "Talk it over with Michael," he said. "In fact, talk it over with Shaner. Bill will be a big help to you." He knew that if he could get both Margot and Michael to include Shaner in major discussions, they would come to rely on the other man as they relied on him.

Margot did not respond, merely stared vacantly at him. *Too much for her right* now Benton thought. He decided to wait a few days and again outline the steps that would need to be taken for the journey. He also would need to try and find the right time to talk with her once again about one of their main problems — Anna.

Chapter Seventeen

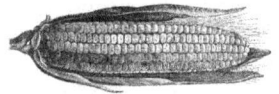

*A*ll members of the group, even the youngest, pitched in for the upcoming journey. The remaining bread and dry food was packaged as best they could and set aside for the trip. The tribe did as Benton had suggested and consumed only the food that was still in the tin cans. All four males, including Jamie, were out each day trapping or hunting and managed to supply a small amount of extra rations for immediate consumption. "Enough to keep body and soul together," Benton said as they finished a sparse evening meal. Everyone gave him surprised looks. "An old saying. I remember my grandmother used to say it."

"When you were short of food?" Lucille asked.

"No! No! We were never short of food," Benton replied. He really had no explanation for his comment. "We always had plenty of food. More than we could possibly eat. I don't know why my grandmother said it. I guess it was just something to say," he finished lamely, shaking his head.

"Oh," was all Lucille said, and only Shaner added to her comment, stating, "I don't think I've ever heard that before either."

I guess I haven't realized how much older I am than the rest of them Benton thought. *I just assume that they'll understand what I say. It's just an old saying, but they must not have any old sayings – or jokes. I don't recall any of them ever telling or making a joke.* He looked around at the other faces, all so serious. *They don't laugh much either. I guess they don't have much to laugh about.*

"It's not important:" Benton responded to Shaner. "Just making small talk," but he wondered if the group would know what he meant by *small talk*.

Everyone was silent for a few minutes until Jamie exclaimed, "Mr. Benton, you need to tell us some more about the time when you were little."

Benton smiled at the boy, relieved for a moment to be off the topic of food. He thought it odd that everyone referred to Shaner as Bill while the rest called him Mr. Benton. Even Margot and Michael had never called him Amos, and he had almost forgotten that he had a given name. *Wonder if it's because I'm older or because I appear more threatening.* He spent a great deal of time with Margot and imagined that they had developed a good rapport. Sometimes he caught her looking at him when she thought he was unaware, and he speculated on whether she saw him as a potential mate. If she did, he would not find it unacceptable. In fact, he thought the idea rather agreeable. It had been years since he was at all interested in a woman, not since Martha's psychiatric illness. He was fully aware that Margot had become somewhat dependent on him, consulted him about almost any issue before a decision was made. She also provided an update every day on the progress being made for the move. *We'd make a good team, be able to keep everyone focused on survival* he mused. *Might be a nice way to continue my life . . . not have to follow the rules of tower living.*

Benton looked over at Margot who was giving him a quizzical look since he had not replied to Jamie's question. "Everything's going along okay, isn't it?" she asked anxiously. "We're nearly set for the journey south, and everyone is very excited about it. I'm certain we will all find a new place to live that we'll like."

Benton smiled, acknowledging her comments. He knew the time was coming when he would have to tell her that he would not complete the journey with the group.

"We have two very serious things to discuss, Margot," Benton said as he drew her away from the others. "The trek has to start in the next few days as it is getting warmer. Let's you and I go outside for a few minutes so we can have a discussion without input from everyone else."

"All right," Margot said, but he could see a hint of suspicion in her eyes.

The two made their way out of the haven, and both could see it was a rather pleasant afternoon. Although there was a cool breeze, bushes and trees were showing buds, and the air smelled of spring and warmer weather. When they settled on the side of the embankment far north of the toilet, Benton pointed out that the stream was now free of ice. "Good time to get going," he said.

"Why are we here?" Margot asked, looking intently into his face. She liked being out in the sun and liked being alone with Benton, without everyone else watching and listening. Still she was curious as to why they had to leave the others.

This is not going to be easy Benton thought. *I hope she will be reasonable, doesn't just get up and run back into the haven.*

Finally, he said, "We need to leave the haven tonight, and Anna will have to be left behind."

Margot didn't reply, merely stared at him and then, as he had expected, started to get up.

"Please listen to me," Benton pleaded as he pulled her back beside him. "We discussed this possibility at least two months ago. You simply can't take her with you. She will be too big a burden as she will have to be watched constantly. None of you will survive if you take her along. Is that what you want?"

"No, No," Margot began to sob, tears streaming down her face. Benton had never seen her this way – not even when Robin had died. "She's one of us, one of the family. How can I leave her?"

"It's not whether you can leave her, Margot. That's no longer an issue. The issue is how best to accomplish the feat."

"Shoot her?" Margot's voice rose, and she gave him a look of loathing. "Shoot her like you shoot those deer? Is that what you want? She's one of us. You just want me to kill her?"

"No, No," Benton said again as he tried to soothe the sobbing woman. If he could get Margot to stop crying, he might be able to have a rational discussion with her. "Help me here. Help me think of some way to help Anna."

After a few minutes Margot's sob subsided but were replaced with a low keening sound as she rocked back and forth. He knew the woman was facing one of the hardest decisions she might ever have to make, and he knew not to say anything more. He merely took her hand and rubbed it, trying to soothe the hurt. He knew he could not help her make the decision. That had to be hers alone – or possibly with Michael. He also knew that Margot would finally realize that Anna would have to be left behind.

The two sat silent for nearly a half hour as the sun moved further into the western sky. Margot shivered slightly and then looked squarely at Benton. "All right. I can see you are not talking about shooting her, and I guess I've known since you first mentioned this a while ago that Anna would be left behind. Now, what can be done so that she won't know . . . so that the others won't ever know. If they found out we'd killed her, they couldn't be sure that wouldn't be their fate at some other time."

Benton was relieved that Margot had finally come to accept the situation. "When no one's hovering on top of us, let's you and I . . . Michael, if you wish . . . look at the medicines Shaner and I dug out of the ruined part of the haven. No one seems to know their use, but we have those few books the elders brought into the haven, and they are mostly on survival. I'm fairly certain the usage for some of those pills will be listed in those pages. Some of them must be sedatives that we can give to Anna."

"So we would just give her the pills the night we leave," Margot asked. "She'll just go to sleep and never wake up. There won't be any pain?"

"Right," Benton responded, relieved that Margot seemed to have accepted the solution put forth for Anna. He wasn't certain the woman would just go to sleep without any distress. He knew nothing about sedatives and felt there was a good possibility that the woman would awaken, find herself alone and simply stay in the haven and starve to death. She might even wander outside, hurt herself and lie alone in the woods waiting to die. However, he did not express any of these doubts to Margot. Quickly he said, "I'll give Anna the pills so you won't have to do it. You, Michael and I, with a great deal of help from Shaner and Noreen, will get the group on their way. There'll be a lot of confusion getting everyone loaded with their backpacks and getting them herded the way we'll need to go. It'll be dark, and probably no one will notice that Anna is not with us. After we've gone a couple of miles, you mention this, and I'll volunteer to go back and get her."

"You'll give her the pills then?" Margot asked. "You wouldn't just go off and leave her by herself . . . to starve?"

"Of course not," Benton replied. "How could you think that? In fact, it might be a good idea to give her a couple of pills late in the afternoon the day we plan to leave. No one pays too much attention to her anyway except to be certain she's fed and cleaned up now and then, so if she's extra quiet, it may just seem her normal way of acting."

The explanation Benton had provided seemed to mollify Margot, and they soon returned to the haven. That evening just at dusk the group was told that they would be leaving in a few minutes and to get their packs ready to go. There was a flurry of activity. Everyone gathered their belongings and made certain they took as much food as each could carry. One morning several days earlier Michael had slipped back to Mrs. Yates' house and in a rubbish pile had located an old child's wagon, dilapidated and with two wheels missing. Using part of a door in the haven, he and Benton had put together a makeshift cart which could be loaded with some supplies and pulled along. Both of the two men knew the cart could not withstand the whole journey, but it would be of help during the first few days.

Shaner and Michael carried the two rifles that had been captured with the Bureau men the past autumn. An old pistol that had belonged to the elders was tucked in the pocket of Benton's heavy jacket. He wanted the group to leave immediately for he knew that without their usual night's sleep, everyone would be exhausted the next morning from walking all night over unknown terrain. That guaranteed that they would sleep soundly all the next day, hidden from any sustainers who might already be in the fields.

About halfway through the night when they had gone several miles, Margot suddenly stopped, looked around and exclaimed, "Where's Anna?

"She must have lagged behind," Benton quickly said. "Did any of you keep an eye on her?" There was no response so he continued, "Well, the rest of you go on ahead. I'll circle back and find her. Here, Bill, take my pack. I know it's heavy, but I'll travel faster without it. We'll catch up with you – Anna and me"

Margot got the group moving again, and Benton headed back to the haven. When he got there, he discovered that Anna was still sedated. He sat by her side on her pallet, wondering what she had been like before the accident. She was not unattractive with her heavy blonde hair and pale complexion although inactivity had led to a slackening of her body, and tiny wrinkles could be seen at the edge of her eyes. He thought that originally she might have been very personable and easygoing with a good sense of humor that probably would have been a great benefit to the elders. Now she had become a major liability to the group. She lay before him – her eyes closed, her breathing shallow. He knew he couldn't just leave her there and take the chance that she would awaken and suffer alone in the cold and darkness. Quickly he pulled out the pistol and placed it against her head. The sound of the shot reverberated off the haven walls.

At first, since they had been outside so infrequently, all of them tended to stumble over the slightest impediment – tree roots, clumps of grass, slight indentations in the ground – and the wobbling of the flimsy cart predicted an early breakdown. Finally, it dawned on Benton. They were traveling at night; sustainers would not be out and about; the roads would be free and clear for travel. Once they moved onto the roads and particularly when the moon was full, they covered several miles each night. It had taken Benton a night of hard travel to catch up with the group after he returned to the haven, and he was impressed and pleased at how speedily they were moving through the unfamiliar territory.

"Had a little problem with Margaret and Connie keeping up," Shaner said, referring to the two youngest members," but Michael and I took turns carrying their packs part of the way. Gave them a little rest."

"Otherwise, everything is fine," Margot put in. "We seem to be covering a good amount of ground, and we've only glimpsed a few sustainers during the day."

"The fields will be full of them shortly," Benton said. "Planting time is here, and all the empty land will be tilled. We'll have to be extra careful as the sun is up earlier, so we'll have shorter nights in which to travel. That means it will take us longer to reach our destination, wherever that is."

"Where's Anna?" Noreen suddenly asked.

Benton took his time answering. "I don't know for certain," he said. "I went back toward the haven but couldn't find her. I even went back as far as the haven, but it was empty. I think she just wandered off as we were moving, and we didn't notice until it was too late." He couldn't meet Margot's eyes. "I'm not certain she was up to the trek anyway . . ." He let the sentence dangle and then continued. "At any rate, we certainly can't go back now to try and find her. Besides we have no idea in which direction she might have gone."

The group was quiet for a few minutes, and there was a sniffle or two since Anna had been with them physically if not mentally. If Margot wondered what Benton had done about Anna, she didn't ask – only said a few words of comfort and got the group settled down to sleep. As far as Benton could tell, Anna's name was never mentioned again, and they continued moving southward.

The days grew warmer, and the clan's clothing became a problem. It was heavy and too hot. However, as complaints grew, Michael said, "Listen to me! You can't leave your coats and sweaters behind. First of all, a sustainer might stumble across them. Second, you're gonna need them when next September comes, no matter where we end up. Even when we get to the Gulf of Mexico, it will be cold during the winter months." He didn't say "if we get to the Gulf" as he wished to keep the group's spirits high. Sometimes late at night when he couldn't get to sleep, he had doubts about their survival chances. However, he never expressed these thoughts. If Margot and Benton had misgivings, they also kept quiet. On the other hand Shaner was the height of optimism, striding confidently over the terrain, sometimes whistling. Unlike the others, he seemed never to tire and never complained.

They were fortunate in one respect. When the cities and towns had been razed and turned into farm land, the forests were left intact. No one, even Benton, could recall why this was so.

"For the animals," Shaner had suggested.

"Doubt it, Bill." Benton shrugged out of his pack as they settled for the day in a grove of willows. "You notice how trees all seem to border a stream or like these, a rocky outcrop. Might have been harder to plow them under, but I imagine it had something to do with the total environment. I'm not certain what would occur if the entire country was mowed down from ocean to ocean like a floor."

"So, the trees help out the people in the towers?" Lucille interrupted.

"I don't know how to answer that," Benton replied thoughtfully. "People in the towers seldom ever get out to where trees are. Of course, there are trees in the towers, a few in selected spots mostly in huge pots. There are also some in tower arboretums so that people young and old know what trees are."

He simply didn't know the answer to Lucille's question, but after a minute of silence he continued. "Lot of people used to use trees for firewood, like old Mrs. Yates. But that isn't the case now. They are kept as a refuge for animals, I guess, like the ones Michael and I trapped or shot. For us," he added, "they are a godsend. Look how lucky we are this morning to have a place to hide and where we are somewhat protected from the elements."

What am I talking about he thought. *I don't know why forests are still needed or why they weren't razed. There are probably all kind of reasons. Why do they keep asking me all of these questions? Why do I keep trying to provide them with information – answer all of their innumerable queries?* Then he realized the answer. He was the oldest. He had lived both before and after Babel-ON. He had become their encyclopedia.

Chapter Eighteen

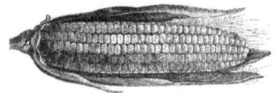

$\mathcal{W}$ ithout a calendar, Benton was not certain of the month. He knew they had been traveling for approximately ten weeks, but one night just seemed to run into another. After leaving the southern part of Iowa, they had crossed the Mississippi River at the beginning of the second week without any problem. As with the roads, all rail lines and bridges had been kept in good repair for food transportation to the towers. Since the group traveled only at night with no sustainers out and about, they easily crossed any rivers in their path south. The days were much longer now, and Benton judged by the size of the crops in the fields near the woods that it was at least July.

The group's original food supply had been exhausted several weeks earlier, and all had suffered some weight loss. Fortunately, they had located some fields of early vegetables – peas, green beans, onions, radishes – being careful to leave as little trace of their gleaning as possible. All of these had to be eaten raw and consumed in very small quantities for fear of stomach problems or for fear that a sustainer might notice an unusually large amount of missing food. Benton and Michael set traps each morning before sleep, but as expected most animals were not out in daylight. They had caught a number of rabbits but were so fearful of having a sustainer see a fire on which to cook them that they had tossed the animals aside.

"Will we ever have anything hot to eat again?" Michael grumbled as he crunched on a radish. "I can't even remember what hot tea tastes like."

Several other grumbles echoed his comments. Benton noted that Margot never seemed to get upset at the fussing over lack of food, griping about being dirty, or whining about bites from various insects. He was amazed at her composure and her ability to energize them to continue the journey. She was their true leader, the one they accepted as able to make the correct decisions, the one who would take them to safety. However, he knew he would have to talk to her within the next couple of weeks and force her to accept a very necessary change in her plans.

"Let's walk out to the edge of that field," Benton said to Margot one morning as only a faint glow of color showed in the morning sky. Sustainers were still in huts, so Benton knew they would not be observed for approximately an hour. The air was quite humid, and Benton surmised that by now they must be in central Texas. A night before, they had passed a field of cotton, but other than Benton no one had ever seen the crop, not even Shaner.

"You're wearing some of it," Benton said, pointing to their clothing. "You don't eat it. It's processed, goes through a process that turns it into fibers, thread, cloth from which to make things. You wouldn't be wearing much if there hadn't been any cotton . . ." He had let his words drift away as he could see the attitude of the group was that if one couldn't eat it, why have it.

Margot and Benton stopped at the edge of the field and looked at the neat rows of plants, thriving in the rich soil. "Soy beans, I think," Benton said, quick to add, "not beans that you can just pick and eat raw like we've been doing. They'd make you sick."

Margot merely smiled and stared into the distance. Her face was pale, and he noted that her nose appeared sharper than when he had first seen her. Long matted hair curled around her shoulders as did that of the others. They had with them some shears and a few other tools taken from the haven, but cutting hair or any form of grooming seemed to take too much energy. *I'm sure I look as bad to her* Benton thought. *Scraggly beard, long hair, and I know I don't smell too good. None of us do.*

"It's lovely out here, isn't it?" Margot asked. "Peaceful and quiet, just like in the haven."

Benton wasn't certain how to respond. He had been able to feel the uncertainty of the group when they had to start the trek. Even though it had been difficult living after the accident, they had felt secure. Now so much was new, and the fear of the unknown stretched before them. "Yes, it is peaceful, I'll give you that," Benton replied.

As far as they could see, rows of plants stretched their leaves upward, awaiting the sun's warming rays. Suddenly a fine mist drifted toward them as the irrigation system began its early morning ritual. The fact that most fields were well-irrigated helped the group immensely. While food was scarce, water was plentiful, at least for drinking. All they had to do was put out a couple of containers on the edge of a field, and they would shortly be filled with water. Of course, they had to be careful that the containers would not be discovered, but so far that had not been a problem.

During the past weeks of travel, the relationship between Margot and Benton had deepened. She had noted and spoken with him about the attachment of Shaner and Noreen. "Once we're settled in the new place, wherever and whenever that will be, Michael will become involved with one of the other older girls. Even Jamie is at the age where he will be with someone in the not too distant future. That's the way it should be and the way it has to be. We will need additional members."

Although Margot had not said anything about the two of them, Benton knew that she expected that they would eventually mate and would stay as the leaders of the group. That would not only provide continuity but would insure that there would be a sense of order. In that way the group would be able to grow larger, provide support for each other and survive.

Throughout the tedious trek as they journeyed south, the group had skirted the huge towers at Kansas City, Wichita, and Dallas as well as numerous smaller sub-towers. It would not be too many days before the Houston tower would loom on the horizon. Benton knew he would have to be away from the group much before that time — far enough away that the Bureau could not trace them. Quietly he began to explain the immediate problem they faced.

"Margot, we've been fortunate so far. No one has been too sick or gotten too injured to keep going. Oh, we've had a couple of close calls, but nothing to complain about. Now we've got to decide how we are going to be able to set up a new haven without being caught."

"What do you mean? We'll find a place beside a stream and build a place into the bank – just like the haven."

"Sounds easy when we talk about it," Benton said, "but the reality is that you will be lucky to survive next winter. Hopefully you can find some place near the Gulf. By place I mean a cave or series of caves to live in. I doubt if you will have time to dig a haven. Plus building material. What will you do for building material? You can't just order up wood and concrete. It must have taken your grandparents and parents months — years maybe – to get the old haven habitable."

"I realize . . . have always realized that it won't be easy, but we'll make it work. We'll look for where an old sustainer house stood. There may be a . . ." Margot stopped for a minute, searching for the right word, "a cellar, I think you called it. We could survive in that as the winter won't be as cold as it was in the north."

"Well, if you can find such a place." Benton thought that might be a possibility, and he knew that the temperature would not be as severe the farther south the group ventured. Still, the winter months would be cold and with much more moisture the closer they got to the water.

"There'll be more food, too," Margot said. "More and varied. Wild plants – fruit, nuts, berries – much more than in Iowa. You said so yourself. You said there would be orchards of fruit and nuts and fields with root vegetables. We will steal from the fields and hunt everything we can find in the surrounding areas. We'll store it and ration ourselves. Maybe we can get some fish, of course at night when we can't be seen. You, Michael, Bill and even Jamie can trap and hunt for us."

"I won't be with you," Benton said quietly.

"What? What are you talking about? Of course, you'll be with us. You're one of us now. I've grown used to you. I need you. We all need you." Margot's voice had risen, and Benton tried to quiet her.

"Shhh, shhh," let me explain. He put his arm around her shoulders and drew her close to him, but she would not be quiet.

"I don't understand what you are saying. You're the one who got us out of the haven. You've made sure we have gotten this far. You've taught us so much, taught us things we needed to know. How can you say you won't go with us?" She was panting a little, and Benton knew that shortly she would be crying.

"Margot, listen to me, please." He held her closer, pushing the locks of hair back from her face. "Give me a minute to explain what I said. Remember, you're our leader. You need to know what's going on . . . what's probably going to happen."

After a few minutes he felt her relax in his arms. It was growing lighter, and he knew sustainers soon would be coming out to the field. Very shortly they would need to move back into the safety of the trees and bushes where the rest of group was probably already asleep.

"The Bureau will come looking for Shaner and me. They would have found our truck parked where we left it last August. By now they have already been talking to Mrs. Yates about our disappearance. Of course, you and I both know that the old woman won't give us away. I've never met other people as good as her who could say they don't know anything. Especially who could say that and be believable. She'll just tell them that we were staying in her old place when she returned to her sub-tower. So, we're safe with her, but the Bureau people won't simply give up and go away. Not my boss Solomon John, if I know him. And I do know him. He's tenacious . . .

and suspicious. He'll want to know what happened to Shaner and me"

"But you'll be gone," Margot interrupted. "He won't find you."

"I know, Margot, but John will have the men from the Bureau comb every inch of those fields. They know they should at least find our bodies, bones from our bodies. Eventually, they'll discover the haven."

"Oh," Margot looked at him.

"Yes, oh," Benton said, "and when they find the haven, they'll find the little bit of furniture, pots . . . whatever." He was careful not to mention that they would also find Anna's body. "They'll know someone was able to live there and is now gone. They – Solomon John – won't rest until he solves the mystery."

"But we're so far away now," Margot began. "We're miles and miles away. He won't know which way we went or whether any of us survived."

"True, we are far away, but are we far enough? If I were hunting the group I'd look in this direction. I'd assume, just like I've done, that you might survive where the climate would be somewhat milder. I'd send out people to hunt for you all across the southern part of the country. Remember, the weather's good now, and the Bureau people could get food from the sustainers. They don't have the same problem that we do trying to find something to eat. Wouldn't take them long and they'd probably track us."

"You're just trying to frighten me," Margot began to protest.

"No, Margot. You know better than that. You know what I'm saying is true. If you want the group to be able to stay together and survive outside a tower, you are going to have to do what I tell you."

"What? What must I do?

Benton was silent for another few minutes. Then he took her face in his hands, noting the fear in her blue eyes. Thoughts flooded his mind. *She knows. She doesn't want to face it, but she knows. They have to leave me behind and go on by themselves. If they don't, all of this will be for nothing. They'll either be killed trying to get away or they'll be taken captive, put in a tower . . . or even worse.*

"You and I will make some plausible excuse and leave the group. Shaner and Michael are capable of taking the others and continuing south. We will walk at least two days, maybe three, away from the group in a different direction. Let's say we walk toward New Mexico. Whoever is following will, hopefully, assume we're all heading for California. That would be a good assumption."

"Then what?" Margot asked. "Where do we go so they can't find the two of us?"

This was the hard part. He knew Margot would put up innumerable objections, but he knew his plan was the only one that would work – possibly work was more like it. She would have to follow along with it.

"You will have to leave me wherever we decide to stop," Benton said. "It can't be so far away that you won't be able to rejoin the group if you travel as fast as you can, but it must be far enough away that no one will immediately start looking for you as well as me. You will have to cover a lot of ground and then when you rejoin the group have them move as fast as possible.

"But won't the people from the tower question you? Won't they be able to find out about us?"

"Yes, they will question me when they do find me, eventually, after a couple of days. I'll crawl as far as I can from where you leave me, put as much distance as I can between the clan and me. When they do find me, I'll be unable to say exactly where or why I was abandoned. Obviously, I'll be injured. Also, I'll be sick, probably out of my mind. My responses to any questions will be fuzzy, ambiguous, vague . . . When I'm finally well enough to explain, I'll still act uncertain. I'll give them something, some explanation that most will find feasible . . ." He let the sentence hang.

"I don't understand," Margot insisted. "If I leave you some place away from the group, and you are found five or six days later, will you be able to feign illness enough to be believable?"

"It won't all be pretense, Margot. After five or six days outside in a field, continually in the hot summer sun, maybe even a little rain, I'll really be ill . . . ill enough that what I say should be believable."

"How are you going to do that?" Margot looked at him in disbelief. "How can you make yourself that sick?"

"I won't do it, Margot. You will," Benton said softly. "You will have to leave me, and I mean leave immediately and return to the others," Benton paused, "after you shoot me!"

Epilog

*T*hey found him in a field of alfalfa near a sustainer tower in the western part of Texas. A group of sustainers disembarking from their trucks to prepare for the day's labor had stumbled across him – dehydrated, his clothes in tatters, his hair matted and dirty, his thigh scarred and festering from a bullet wound, his left arm hanging grotesquely at his side. Mumbling and raving, he had been rushed to medical aid at a nearby sub-tower, treated and put in a hospital bed.

"Well, Benton, have a pleasant journey?" Benton focused on the voice. It was Solomon John. For an instant Benton thought the question was a serious one but then decided it was John's attempt at a joke. Still you never knew with John.

"Where am I? When did you find me?" Benton's eyes darted about bewildered, questioning. "Am I back at Babel-ON? How did you . . . save me?"

"Save you?" Solomon John snorted. "We thought you had decided to become one of them. Those still outside."

"I did. I became one of them." Benton grimaced, watching the eyes of Solomon John widen. "I had to join them, or I wouldn't have been able to get free. I wouldn't be here now . . . alive . . . wherever here is . . ." He made an attempt to sit up but collapsed back onto the bed.

"Where's Shaner?" another voice interrupted, and Benton could see that not only the Manager of the Bureau of Sustenance but several other men were in the room. Even the Director was there.

"Dead," he said, his voice choking. "Dead. Several months ago . . . in the late winter, I think. Around January or early February. Was hard to keep track of time . . ." He signed deeply and then slightly rising looked directly at Solomon John. "And it's our fault. Our fault. We killed him."

John started and quickly glanced at the others in the room. Benton could see the irritation in his face. "What do you mean we killed him? Do you mean . . . what are you saying? You must mean those others that were with you . . . them?"

"No!" Benton hesitated, taking his time breathing slowly, gasping a little, making every word an effort. "I mean you and me — the Bureau. We were too sure nothing was out there. We said they all had been accounted for, all moved inside. You didn't really think anything, anyone possibly could be found . . . remember? You said no one could be living outside – no one." He looked from John to the Director. "We had no experience with anything . . . anyone like them. They caught us, kept us prisoners, made us live like they were living – animals living underground. Poor Shaner. He was lost right from the start; he was a towerite, couldn't adapt, couldn't eat the rotten food what little there was of it. It was different for me. I had lived before the towers. At least I knew how it had been. No matter what we think, we shouldn't send a man out to meet them if he's had no experience, no training . . ." His voice faded, and he sank back on the bed.

"I don't understand. Do you mean that because he couldn't adjust, they actually killed him . . . just to be killing him?" Solomon John's eyes widened. "My God, we're dealing with savages. Savages!"

"No! No!" Benton responded quickly. "It's our fault, didn't prepare him. But they might as well have killed him. He'd have suffered less. He couldn't adjust to the lack of adequate food, the hard traveling when we moved out of the sanctuary, the heavy load he had to carry . . . he tried to escape twice while we were moving on across country. They caught him . . . kept him tethered with a rope . . . whipped him. He died . . . just finally gave up and died . . . killed . . . all gone now. . . all gone." Benton let his voice drop; his eyes closed. He waited; his breathing became more regular.

Solomon John watched him closely. "What do you mean . . . just died? They whipped him to death?"

"I think he's back asleep, sir," the medical attendant began when there was no response from Benton. "He's been under heavy sedation for pain ever since he was found early yesterday morning. He may not be able to answer any more questions for several hours."

"Let's all go into one of the conference rooms," the Director suggested as he moved toward the door. "Let him get some rest. Then he may be better able to answer our questions. Remember," he motioned the attendant to his side for emphasis, "no one in here without official permission. Understand, no one!"

The attendant nodded and the rest of the men slowly filed out. Benton lay motionless, only continuing to moan slightly as the orderly adjusted his bedding. The orderly waited a few moments and then left the room.

Did they believe him? Benton's mind wandered as he went over the few minutes of John's interrogation. *He had tried to be careful, so careful. Had not told how many individuals there were in the group. Had given them some information but not too much. John, he knew, was hard to convince. You could never tell whether he believed you . . . could never tell what he was thinking. Benton was fully aware of Solomon John's suspicious nature . . . always on the watch for a careless word, always ferreting out hidden meanings. He also was aware of John's antagonism toward him, even though the man tried to cover it up. Well, he would use the pretense of drifting into and out of sleep to continue collecting his thoughts for the next sessions, and there would be other sessions, many if John had his way. He wondered if they would move him back to Babel-ON and decided that they would. Could he pretend to have a relapse . . . make it take longer to get coherent information from him. That was a possibility. He felt he could fake a relapse. Who could say it wasn't true?*

Although it had been difficult to get Margot to come to grips with the fact that she would have to shoot him, Benton could recall her pointing the gun and firing. He had not realized how badly being shot would hurt and remembered Anna alone in the twilight of the haven. He had nearly passed out from the pain as he struggled to get up off the ground and clear his head. By then Margot was gone, as he had instructed. He knew she would have to convince Shaner to stay with the group instead of come looking for him as he thought his partner would wish to do.

A few minutes after Margot had shot him, he had realized that he would not be able to stand and slowly began to crawl, dragging his bleeding leg between the rows of plants, and heading away from where Margot had stood. He was not certain how many days and nights he had crawled, but it seemed like an eternity. He alternated between bouts of chills which made his body tremble and streams of sweat which seeped down his neck and soaked his clothing. Finally, he had merely given up and waited – hoping to be discovered.

Benton tried to move his arm. While it wasn't painful, it felt strange. It was in some sort of contraption that kept it immobile, and he tried to recall how it had been injured. *Arm probably got broken when I fell on it* he thought. He hoped that he was not so badly disabled that he would not fully recover, but he knew that he had to appear to have been left for dead. He had emphasized that fact to Margot. Anything less and Solomon John would have him up on charges, dismissed from the Bureau and, possibly, incarcerated. He would be questioned again and again in the next few days. Of that he was certain, and he would give them, particularly Solomon John, a little bit more information each time. He would take his time – explain how they had been captured and taken to the haven in one session, emphasize how he and Shaner had suffered from the cold and hunger pangs, recall he and Shaner trying to plan an escape. If pressed, he would come up with a few names and say that once he had overheard the group talking about California. He would do everything possible to confuse Solomon John and foil any attempt by the Bureau to locate his friends.

His friends. The thought made him smile. *They were his friends now . . . would always be his friends. Maybe in a few months*

... *no, it would take a few years at least to be trusted ... before Solomon John would give up his suspicions, before he would be permitted outside Babel-ON again. Maybe he could find where the group had gone, could see if all or any had survived their trek, would find out if they would welcome him ...* He could feel the effects of the drugs given him by the orderly. Soon he would be asleep and not have to think about the others. As he drifted off, he thought of Margot and hoped that somewhere far distant on the trek she would be thinking of him.

CPSIA information can be obtained
at www.ICGtesting.com
Printed in the USA
LVHW030801310719
625977LV00001BA/12